HIGHLANDS CHRISTMAS

WISHES COME TRUE

AMY QUICK PARRISH

FLYING CACTUS

CHAPTER 1

*S*now fell lightly on a cozy upscale home decorated in full Christmas splendor: candles glowed in the windows, icicle lights twinkled on the roof, white lights danced around tall pine trees and sparkled on the bushes. On the front door a huge balsam wreath with a giant red bow and sparkling lights welcomed visitors.

Through the bay window, a group of guests shared food around a dinner table as laughter filled the air. A fire roared below a mantle covered in greenery and the rest of the home was decked out to the nines with poinsettias, greenery and ornaments. A tiny Christmas village with a toy train running through it filled the bay window.

The dining room table was decorated in a festive tablecloth, with reindeer napkin rings, and in the center of it all – and quite out of place, a rather garish centerpiece of a tacky toy squirrel with a bowl of (actual) shelled walnuts.

"Who's having another slice of pie?" asked the hostess, Melissa Mackenzie, dressed in a red sweater and a green and red plaid skirt. She held up a perfect, tempting slice. Everyone shook their heads no.

"Dave?" Melissa asked her balding husband, who was ignoring her and speaking to a younger, vivacious blond to his right. "Dave? How about another slice of pie?"

Dave looked up, slightly annoyed. "I'm stuffed."

Melissa held out a slice toward the woman Dave was speaking to. She was her brother's ex and a friend, so Dave had convinced her that Samantha would be lonely this time of year and they should invite her since her brother couldn't attend.

"Samantha?"

Samantha plastered on a grin and shook her perfectly styled blond hair.

"I'd be so fat I—" She paused and put a hand over her mouth as Melissa frowned and adjusted her sweater over her middle. "I mean, I just couldn't. Right now," finished Samantha.

"I've got a whole other pie in the kitchen. I'll send everyone home with a slice," said Melissa.

The guests, still glassy-eyed from their food comas, reacted: somewhere between happy anticipation and overwhelmed guilt.

Melissa began to clear the plates and two friends followed her into the kitchen to help.

"Oh, really, I can do it," said Melissa.

They insisted and Melissa accepted their help.

"How about a little Christmas music?" Melissa asked.

"It's still Thanksgiving weekend," Dave complained.

"I'll play the snow-related, family songs then."

She planted a loving kiss on Dave's cheek, but he brushed past her and turned back to the football game in the living room.

"Oh, that's right. The game."

There was a slight rustling sound in the walls. Melissa froze for a second. Dave banged on the wall. He banged again.

"Those squirrels—"

Melissa shook her head and returned to the kitchen, cranking up the volume on the music with songs such as "There's No Place Like Home for the Holidays," "Let it Snow" and "Winter Wonderland."

Melissa was in her element humming, sometimes singing along with the music as guests took a part in washing, wiping, drying ... It was a warm, merry vibe and Melissa loved it.

"Melissa, I love what you've done with this place. I remember the kitchen when you first bought it. And the dining room – what a transformation!" her friend, Carol, gushed.

"Thanks. Well, with a degree in interior design I may as well put myself to good use!"

As people began to leave, Melissa handed them

beautifully wrapped Martha Stewart-worthy packages of leftovers, complete with red tartan bows on top.

"Melissa, this is stunning. You shouldn't have," said another.

"Oh, it's nothing. I just love Christmas time. Anything to make it last. Luckily we still have three more weeks."

"Thank you."

As the guests left, she noticed Dave hugged Samantha a little longer than necessary. Melissa felt a pit in her stomach, but shook it off and walked over to hug Samantha herself.

"Thanks so much for being here, Samantha. I know it's been such a hard year for you after your breakup with Ted."

Samantha looked up. "What? Oh. Right. Ted." Somehow in the seconds between the hugs she had managed to tie her scarf in a perfect loose knot. Melissa noticed how together Samantha looked. So odd, considering the garish hostess gift she'd given…

"And thank you for the, uh… nut basket. It's lovely." Melissa gestured toward the hideous basket filled with shelled nuts and a giant, ugly plush squirrel. It just didn't look like something anyone with Samantha's sense of style would give.

"I just saw it and thought of you," said Samantha as she slipped on stylish black boots.

Melissa snapped back into gracious host mode, plastering on the best smile she could as she helped the guests with their coats.

· · ·

WITH THE DISHWASHER humming and the last guests driving away, Melissa plopped down on the couch in front of the crackling fire and cozied under a wool tartan blanket. Dave shuffled in. There was another rustling sound in the walls. He banged on the wall.

"I'll call the squirrel guys again. This is ridiculous," he said.

Melissa was still lost in her thoughts. "What a wonderful party. I'm so glad everyone could make it. It's nice with just the two of us, of course..."

Melissa lifted the blanket - an invitation for Dave to cozy up against her, which he ignored.

"Lions lost again," said Dave.

"That's too bad. Come. Sit. I really want to snuggle up and talk to you about—"

"I want to talk to you, too," said Dave.

Melissa flushed with excitement. "I was thinking we should take a trip - maybe somewhere really Christ-massy, like London, Quebec, Paris or what about Norway? I've been doing some research and I think—"

"I want a divorce," said Dave.

Melissa felt like she'd been blindsided by a truck. She couldn't have heard that right.

"What?"

"I was waiting until the party was over," said Dave.

"But what did you—"

"I'm seeing Samantha," said Dave.

"Samantha, who was just here? Samantha, who

dumped my brother? Samantha, who brought that awful squirrel-nut centerpiece?"

"Yes."

It was silent for a few moments as Dave pressed his mouth into a tight line and Melissa tried to process.

"What about Christmas?"

"I'm going to Barbados," said Dave.

"For Christmas? There's no snow."

"Exactly. Melissa, you're the one who likes the snow and the holidays. I'm sick of it. I'm ready to move on. I'm sorry."

"Move on?"

They never travelled anywhere and all of a sudden, he was going to Barbados? With her brother's ex?

As Dave put on his coat, Melissa remained stunned, still processing.

"Where are you going?" she asked.

"To Samantha's. I think it would be a good idea if I'm gone for a few days so you can get your stuff out."

"MY STUFF?"

"The house is in my name. I'm keeping it."

As MELISSA WOKE up she smiled as she saw the snow-lined windowpanes and the cozy Christmas candles in the windows. Then, as she reached for her phone and saw several missed calls, she remembered her reality.

Thank goodness. He's calling back to apologize,

Melissa thought. But the call was from a number she didn't recognize. She pressed play.

"Good morning," a lovely Highlands accent chirped. "This is Colin MacGregor from MacGregor, Stewart and Duncan. I'm phoning about the, uh, matter with your... with Dave. Please ring me at your earliest convenience so that I might know the name of your lawyer."

Melissa sighed. It was real, after all. As the tears welled up, Melissa set the phone down and slowly dragged herself out of bed. She pulled on a cozy plaid bathrobe and slippers and lit a fire. Once it was crackling, she plopped herself in the comfy chair beside the fire and made a phone call.

"Hello? Marty? Oh, fine. And you? I mean, I guess I'm not fine. I need a lawyer and I wonder if you would... Tuesday? Sounds good. And I can give them your name as my representative? Of course." As she hang up, the tears poured out. She tore into a box of tissues and looked outside.

Yesterday's glorious, shimmering snow had turned to soggy wet, black grit over wet leaves. Sheets of cold rain fell. Melissa threw a raincoat over her bathrobe and donned some bright red rain boots. She opened the door shuffled out to the mailbox, unsuccessfully dodging mud puddles and raindrops. She collected the mail and shuffled through the wet leaves and pools of rain back up the walkway to the house.

. . .

BACK IN HER COZY CHAIR, Melissa sorted through the mail - something caught her eye. *'HUME REAL ESTATE ASSOCIATES'.* She looked more closely, noticing the return address: 'Inverness, Scotland'. Melissa didn't know anyone in Scotland, and it seemed like a long way to send marketing spam. She cracked open a very elaborate seal and opened the letter.

Dear Ms. Mackenzie-

We are dreadfully sorry to inform you of the passing of Mr. Stuart Mackenzie this past September. After searching through our records, we have discovered that you are his third cousin once removed and the next of kin.

Please ring us at your earliest convenience to discuss plans for receiving your inheritance - among the items are Greenhill, his Inverness estate.

Unfortunately, the estate is in disrepair. We note that you live in the US. Our company provides the service of liquidating the property and providing you with the proceeds, minus our handling fee.

Please contact us at your earliest convenience to arrange for the liquidation and kindly provide your banking information so we can transfer the funds into your account.

Best wishes,

Archibald Hume, Hume Realty & Associates.

Melissa set the letter down and opened her laptop. She searched for *'Hume Realty Associate's.* A respectable looking website appeared. She searched *'Greenhill - Inverness estate'* and saw a cozy stone home on the banks of what looked like a river. She read the description.

"On Loch Ness! Wow!"

She re-read the letter and glanced back at the photo of the home. She could see what appeared to be a solid foundation – it needed some paint, and the description talked about some other minor updates needed. I can fix that up myself, she thought.

Her phone rang. Without looking to see who it was, Melissa answered.

"Did you get a lawyer?" It was Dave. Ugh. How had she never noticed that terrible tone of voice he always had?

"Good morning."

"Did you get a lawyer, Melissa? Or are you inca-pable?" In college, she was the one who passed all her classes while he was – what was he doing, anyway?

In the distance, Melissa could hear Samantha's voice. "Dave, come back to bed."

"In a minute," Dave called to her. Melissa rolled her eyes. "My lawyer will be out of the country for the holidays, so I need to know if—"

Melissa took a deep breath, held her head up the way she always did right before she closed on a deal for her interior design clients. She smiled. "I have a lawyer. He'll be in touch." She hung up.

Empowered and a bit inspired, Melissa stomped upstairs and into her bedroom.

She pulled a suitcase out of her closet and began to fill it. She heard a squirrelly noise rustling in the walls and banged on the walls. The noise stopped. She got dressed, went to her computer, searched a travel site and a map.

"Inverness. Inverness." She could see an airport there, but all the flights she could find went to Glasgow or Edinburgh. "Edinburgh it is! And I'll have a lovely train ride afterwards."

She clicked 'COMPLETE ORDER' and snapped her laptop shut.

She got some notepaper and scrawled a quick note. *Good luck with the house.*

Melissa dragged her suitcase down the stairs and put the note on the dining room table next to the dreadful, obnoxious squirrel nut centerpiece.

She opened the door. Several squirrels frolicked in the yard, chasing each other and flickering their tails. She grinned, lumbered back inside and grabbed Samantha's garish nut basket and set it in the doorway.

Melissa made a little squirrel noise to draw their attention. The squirrel closest to her stood up on its hind legs and looked at her. "Yes, you. Come on, in!" Then Melissa flung the front door wide open. She waved at her ride share driver and got into the car. As they drove away, Melissa grinned as she watched a stream of squirrels scuttle into the house.

CHAPTER 2

*M*elissa looked flustered as she dragged her suitcase through the festive terminal. A giant Christmas tree decorated with tinsel and dazzling white lights was in the center of the terminal, and balsam garlands lined the corridors. There were poinsettias at each gate, and even the airline workers wore elf and Santa hats. She stood in a coffee shop line a few feet over from a handsome man in a tweed jacket who was talking on the phone.

"Yes, I'm terribly sorry. It's just that I have some personal business to attend to. So she does have a lawyer? Lovely. And the name is... I see. Perhaps I could ring her myself? Very good. Thank you. And Happy Christmas." The man hung up.

Melissa mocked his charming accent just the tiniest bit. "And a happy Christmas one and all," she whispered to herself.

The man made another phone call. Melissa's phone rang.

"Hello?"

The man in front of her began speaking. "Yes, I'm looking for a Melissa Mackenzie? Terribly sorry, but your husb- er, my client, Dave Foster, needs - I need - the name of your barrister."

They moved up in line. Still on the phone, he attempted to whisper his order. "Yes. A short cappuccino with no foam and—"

"Are you ordering coffee?" Melissa asked into her phone.

The man in front of her turned away from the barista and tried to hold his ear as he spoke into the phone. "Terribly sorry. Yes. I beg your pardon—"

Melissa tapped him on his tweed-covered shoulder. He turned around, startled. He was a dream: a young mix of Sean Connery and Colin Firth with a dash of salt and pepper hair.

She was a bit bedazzled. He was just plain confused.

He pulled his phone away from his ear. "Terribly sorry. Have I taken your spot in the queue?"

"No, I'm on the phone—" Melissa tried to explain.

"Didn't mean to interrupt—" he responded.

Melissa held up her phone and talked into it, exaggerated for his benefit. "Sir? I believe I'm in line behind you. At the airport," she added.

Mortified, the man hung up the phone and looked at her as the barista stared at him.

"That'll be $5.95. Who's next?" asked the barista.

He fumbled for his wallet and paid as Melissa moved forward.

"I'd like a peppermint mocha, low fat, no whip," said Melissa.

"You want whipped cream on that?" asked the barista.

Melissa blinked. "Uh, no. Thank you."

"Name?"

"Melissa."

The barista wrote on the cup and Melissa paid.

The man stood awkwardly as they waited for their coffee.

"So you must be Ms. Mackenzie," he said.

"And you must be Colin MacGregor of MacGregor, Stewart and Duncan," said Melissa.

"I'm sorry."

"It's nothing. It's—"

Tears filled Melissa's eyes and she struggled for a moment. Colin reached into his jacket pocket and handed her a lovely pressed handkerchief.

"Oh. How nice. Old school."

She blew her nose. He looked embarrassed. Melissa looked down at the soiled handkerchief.

"I, uh... I guess I'll be keeping this? I can launder it and get it back—"

"No worries," said Colin.

They stood awkwardly until the coffee arrived. Colin took his. Just as Colin began to wheel away his suitcase, Melissa's coffee arrived with whipped cream and festive sprinkles on top. Melissa looked at it.

"Didn't you order no whip?" asked Colin.

"Well. Yeah. But this is pretty—"

"Miss? My friend here ordered hers with no whip and—"

"She said 'whip'."

"Actually, I distinctly heard her say 'No whip' so since she paid $5.95 for this, you can kindly get her the coffee she requested. Thank you."

Melissa beamed as the barista sighed and made another coffee.

"You're a great lawyer," she said.

"Thank you. I do my best," he said, smiling.

They both paused as they realized they're on opposite sides of the divorce legalities ahead. He held out his hand to shake.

"Lovely meeting you, Ms. Mackenzie."

"And you, Mr. MacGregor. Happy Christmas."

MELISSA MANEUVERED through the aisle toward her seat loaded down with home design magazines, Scotland guidebooks, an iPad, headphones, snacks and a neck pillow. She balanced her coffee precariously as she shuffled into her seat. Just as she began to settle, her seat mate arrived.

Melissa stuffed as much as she could under the seat in front of her and tried to suck in her gut so the passenger could get to her seat. Melissa smiled brightly as the passenger awkwardly tried to pass, but could not. Finally Melissa hoisted herself up, tried to slide out, and knocked into another passenger.

"Sorry," said Melissa.

Melissa slid back into her seat. She began to organize her stuff when another passenger approached to sit just beyond the first one. Melissa repeated the same slide-and-shuffle.

"Please take your seats and fasten your seat belts," said the flight attendant.

"I'm working on it."

Melissa sat down and began to organize. Soon all the magazines, books and iPad were in the seat compartment, her pillow around her neck, her carry on and snacks under the seat. Just as she was about to put on her headphones, the older woman next to her struck up a conversation.

"First time to Scotland?" she asked.

"Yes," Melissa responded.

"Are you on business or pleasure?"

"I - uh..."

"Visiting family?"

"Well, um... Not exactly," Melissa looked ready to cry. She bit her lip, but soldiered on. "I've inherited a home in Inverness."

"Lovely. You're going to check it out and then your husband will join you?"

Melissa smiled. "You know, I'm so exhausted. Time for a little beauty rest. Talk soon." Melissa put on her headphones and eye mask and pretended to sleep.

MELISSA PEEKED through her mask as a cheery flight attendant pushed a cart down the aisle.

"Good morning. Coffee, tea, orange juice?"

"Coffee, please."

"Would you like juice as well?"

"Can I?"

"Of course."

Melissa scrambled to put away all her magazines and headphones as the flight attendant stood with a frozen smile holding the drinks. Melissa finally was able to lower the tray table.

"Sorry," said Melissa, flushing a bit.

"Here you are." The flight attendant handed her the drinks and Melissa accepted them.

Melissa glanced up at the TV map and saw they were over Ireland and nearing Scotland. She looked out the window. It was so green. Gradually, she began to relax and shake away her troubles and replace them with excitement. She was going to have a new life.

CHAPTER 3

*I*n the airport baggage claim, Melissa watched as suitcases began to tumble down the conveyor belt. She reached for hers, lifted it onto the ground and started to walk away but stopped as a voice called her name.

"Mrs. Mackenzie?"

Melissa turned to see Colin MacGregor. He was a bit more rumpled than before, from the flight, but still ruggedly handsome.

"Hi, Colin MacGregor," she said with a smile.

"I believe you have my bag."

"Um. No, this is mine. See?" Melissa bent down to show him the tag. It read 'Colin MacGregor'.

"Oh," she said, feeling her cheeks begin to warm.

"And I have yours." He wheeled an identical suitcase over to her. She took the handle.

"Sorry 'bout that," she said, still flushing.

"No worries. I made the same mistake."

There was an awkward pause.

"I'll... uh... be in touch," Colin said.

"Oh?" Melissa said, confused and a tiny bit hopeful. Then she remembered he was Dave's lawyer and reality came crashing down again. She put on her most neutral, confident smile. "Right. Right. Great. Sure."

Embarrassed, she wheeled her suitcase over toward the taxi lines. Colin trailed right behind her. They stood there as taxis came and went. Melissa took a deep breath and stepped into a taxi, nodding slightly – she hoped neutrally – to Colin as they sped away.

MELISSA LOOKED out the window at the gorgeous city of Edinburgh. She was thrilled.

Beautiful stone buildings, hilly streets, bag pipers playing on the street corners, Edinburgh Castle overlooking it all from atop a hill – it was just breathtaking. And it was all covered in a glistening layer of new snow. On top of that, the city was in full Christmas spirit: pillars covered in greenery, giant wreaths, markets lined with lights and evergreen garlands.

"Look at this! It's straight out of a fairy tale!"

The taxi driver dropped her off at the train station. "Here we are," he said.

"Thank you so much." Melissa tipped him and he helped her with her bag.

At the train station, as Melissa stood in line she noticed another man in front of her had the same bag.

He bought his ticket and turned back, nearly knocking into her – it was Colin.

"Small world," said Melissa, just inches away from him. He smelled like soap and wool.

"Indeed," said Colin, trying to step back. They both nodded to each other and walked away, toward the platform.

MELISSA HOISTED her suitcase onto the train and walked down the aisle to find her seat. As she settled into her seat, she noticed Colin MacGregor had boarded. Melissa held her breath and buried her nose in a novel until he passed her. She breathed a sigh of relief.

Colin came back.

"Apparently I'm 24-A," he said with a nervous grin.

He sat beside her. They both looked uncomfortable and there was a long silence.

Melissa brightened. "You're on holiday, right? That's what they say in the UK?"

"Aye," said Colin. Melissa felt the warmth returning to her cheeks. What an adorable accent.

"So if you're on holiday, it's okay, right? You're just a guy on a train and you happened to sit next to me and you can't work—" A thought occurred to her. "You're not here to spy on me, are you? Do lawyers do that?"

Colin sat up in his chair, offended. "Of course not.

We don't do that. It's just a job. I wanted to be a barrister and family law sounded prosperous, so—"

"Making money from divorces?"

"Well, I—" Colin looked flustered.

"So what brings you here? I see you've got the accent. But you're definitely a New Yorker now, with the—" She saw his reaction and switched course. Good going, Melissa. Way to stereotype a busy lawyer.

"Wow, will you look at this countryside. And those sheep? Amazing."

Colin glanced out the window. "I hadn't missed the sheep."

"I'll let you get back to your work," said Melissa, relieved that at least she had made amends. Melissa turned her gaze toward the window and tried to focus on the scenery rather than the scent of Colin's pine-scented soap.

MELISSA WAS EATING a salad and looking out the window at the Scottish countryside. She had made friends with a middle-aged woman across the aisle and was chatting away.

"This is just the most beautiful country in the world. Of course, I haven't travelled much. Dave, my husband...well, he's soon to be my ex-husband...he never wanted to travel," she said and the woman nodded.

"I'm so sorry."

"It's okay, though. It's going to be okay. He's taking the house, but you'll never believe it. I've inherited a home in Inverness."

"Really? What a wonderful surprise."

"You're telling me! I never even knew the guy, but I'm his long-lost relative. So as soon as I got the letter, I bought a ticket out here to come see it. The company wanted to liquidate it for me and just send me the money, but I've done a lot of home renovations and I needed a ... change. So I thought why not?"

Colin looked over at Melissa.

"That's amazing. And what perfect timing," said the woman.

"I know, right?"

Colin began to look suspicious, but tried to appear focused on his work.

"And you don't even know the deceased? Amazing," said the woman.

"Quite. Forgive me. Might I see that letter?" asked Colin.

Melissa brightened and rummaged through her bag.

"Here it is," she said.

Colin examined the letterhead. He scanned the letter and frowned. "You didn't give them your account information?"

"No. I thought I should just take the house. I'll go to their office and straighten it out, and then I can just move in."

Melissa was beaming, but Colin looked troubled.

"Would you mind, Melissa, if I researched this a bit?" he asked.

"Why would you want to research it?" Her words hung in the air until a thought occurred to her. "Oh, no. Would I have to split this with my husband?"

Colin took a deep breath.

"Not if you wait until you're divorced to accept it. And, actually, you can speak to your barrister and be sure it's only in your name. Or in the name of a child, or even a pet, perhaps."

"Are you allowed to tell me all that?" Melissa asked.

Colin smiled. "I'm on holiday. I'm just chatting with a woman on a train."

Melissa grinned.

"Can you tell me again the name of the company that sent the letter?" asked Colin.

Melissa read from the letter while Colin searched on his laptop. "Hume Real Estate Associates. Inverness, Scotland."

He deftly typed the name and soon found a hit. "Well, they're real," he said.

"Did you think it might not be real?" she asked.

"Sometimes when there's a divorce, scam artists will move in and—"

"Oh, but Dave just asked for the divorce the other night. There's no way a company would have—"

She stopped as she saw Colin's face.

"What?"

He looked down, then back at her. "I've been employed by your husband for several months. We've been working on divorce proceedings for quite some time," he said. Melissa let that sink in. "I'm so sorry," he said, as her eyes began to fill.

"So... since Halloween? All through November. And he... those late nights at work. And he invited her to Thanksgiving. I babysat her kids when she went on that long weekend the same time he had a conference." Melissa's face was beginning to flush and her stomach was in knots.

The woman across the aisle took Melissa's hand. "That's awful."

Even Colin, the callous divorce lawyer sympathized with Melissa. "I'm so sorry," he said again.

"I'm getting a dog and I'm gonna put the house in the dog's name until this is over," Melissa said with determination before she buried her nose in her book in hopes of hiding the tears that were threatening to fall.

CHAPTER 4

$\mathcal{T}$he train rolled to a stop and a sign read 'INVERNESS'.

Melissa got out of her seat. She felt unsteady and nervous, but determined. "Well, this is my stop. Nice meeting you. Both of you," she added.

"It's my stop as well. We seem to be following each other," said Colin.

Melissa smiled and made a show of checking that she had the correct bag. She let Colin pass before she left the train. As she stepped outside the train station, Melissa looked around. Inverness was a relatively modern-looking city but with old-world charm. The River Ness flowed through the city center with Inverness Castle – a much newer castle than what she'd seen in Edinburgh, built with smooth red sandstone on a small hill. Along the river, the bridges and walkways were decorated with greenery, wreaths, and holly, bows and lights. The sound of bagpipes filled the air as a light snow fell.

"You'll find taxis to your left, or a ride share to your right. Very nice meeting you, Ms. Mackenzie. And best of luck," said Colin.

"Thank you. Uh... Happy Christmas?" she said.

"To you, as well," Colin smiled.

His cell rang and he answered, waving as Melissa made her way to the taxi stand.

Inside the taxi, Melissa was excited to begin her journey – that is, until the taxi driver spoke in a thick Highland accent.

"*Càite?*"

"Um, no, I'm Melissa. Nice to meet you," she said.

The taxi driver grinned. "*Aye*, lassie. I said '*Whaur tae*'?" He still had an accent, but at least he was speaking in English. Or Scots. Still, it took Melissa a moment to process.

"Where to? I'm going to Hume Realty and Associates. I have the address," she said, handing him a slip of paper but he dismissed her.

"Never *ye mind, ah ken whaur* that is," he said.

"Oh. Great. Lovely," she said, trying out a new word that seemed more British than 'beautiful'.

The driver began driving. Melissa looked out at the snowy streets and enticing shops while the taxi driver chatted away in a thick Highland accent, which she had a lot of difficulty following. He pointed toward a large castle.

"*This is Caisteal Inbhir Nis, bult' in th' 18th hunner years bit castles ha' staun 'ere sin th' 11th hunner years, mynd. Th' foremaist wis bult' by Malcom III...*"

Melissa had no idea what he was saying, so she did what she often did when Dave talked about work. "That's very interesting..."

"*Aye*, and that's *nae th' hauf o'* it," said the taxi driver.

"Oh?"

"*Aye. Whin Maìri, Queen o' Scots cam tae Inbhir Nis in 1562 she fun th' gates o' th' castle shut against her. Th' clans Fraser 'n' Munroe teuk Inbhir Nis castle fur th' queen, whilk hud refused her admission. Th' queen efter hanged th' governor, a Gòrdan wha hud refused entry.*"

"You don't say..." said Melissa as she tried to pick out words here and there. She got 'Mary, Queen of Scots' and 'castle' and 'refused admission'. And 'hanged.'

She was relieved to see Hume Realty ahead. Melissa's taxi dropped her off. She looked around. The parking lot was empty and it was dark inside the building. She leaned toward the driver, still in his taxi.

"Would you mind waiting just a bit?" she asked.

"*Na kinch*," he responded. Melissa was baffled.

"I'm sorry?"

"*Dinnae be sorry, na fashes. Ah will hauld yer* horses," he said with a twinkle in his eye.

"Well, I'm not in a hurry, I'd just like you to wait a minute, if you wouldn't mind?"

"*Aye*, Lassie. As I've been telling you, *dinna fash yerself*," he repeated.

Taking that as a yes, Melissa walked to the front door and knocked. She knocked again, but given the empty parking lot and the darkness of the windows, she knew she was defeated.

She returned to the taxi.

"They're closed. The house is about twelve miles from here. Maybe I need to rent a car. Do you know any place?"

"*O' coorse. Richt by th' train station. I'll tak' ye straight-away,*" said the driver.

"Oh, thank you," said Melissa.

She sat in silence as the taxi wove through the traffic. At the car rental lot, the driver helped her with her luggage.

"Enjoy your time in Scotland, Miss," he said, clear as day, with a grin.

"But you -- I couldn't underst-- I mean -- Thank you," Melissa said, flustered.

"Just a bit of atmosphere I like to provide to the tourists. Safe travels." He waved as he drove off.

MELISSA GOT into the left side of the car and saw the steering wheel was on the other side. Oops. She scooted herself awkwardly over to the driver's side of the car. Melissa tried to get her bearings. She took a deep breath and looked down. The gear shift was on the left-hand side.

"Oh my gosh. It's a stick." Deep breath, Melissa thought to herself. Then she took out her letter, plugged the address into the GPS, and turned on the ignition. She took another deep breath. *It's just driving... You can do this.* She slowly backed up. She turned. She started going forward and there was another car heading right toward her. She panicked and slammed on the breaks. She let the car in front of her go. Then another car. Then another car. And another car. Finally, when there was no traffic in the street to turn into but a lineup behind her, the car stalled. She started it up again and turned left. But she was still going the wrong way.

Cars leaned on their horns.

"Oh my gosh. Okay. Deep breath."

Melissa turned back into the parking lot and waited. The car stalled again.

Gritting her teeth, she started the car again. She watched the flow of traffic, closed her eyes a moment, then opened them and made the turn. She was doing it!

"Alba gu brath!" Melissa screamed out the only Scottish phrase she knew: Scotland Forever. Beaming, she drove down the correct/wrong side of the street. But now there was a rotary in her path.

"Okay, Mel. You got this," she said, clutching the steering wheel. Gingerly, she turned. For a moment, she was veering straight into oncoming traffic—

"Nope, nope, other way," she told herself as she corrected herself and made her away past the roundabout.

She'd been holding her breath the entire time. She exhaled and continued driving out of Inverness.

MELISSA CLENCHED the steering wheel as she maneuvered down a narrow little road along the River Ness. River Ness... something familiar about that. It finally dawned on her when she saw the sign: Loch Ness! Of course! Delighted, Melissa pulled over and took a selfie in front of the sign.

As she stood and looked out at the deep, dark waters, she could imagine how the stories must have evolved – this was a dark, long stretch of water in a cold, isolated area. Why not come into the warm pub with a fun story to tell your friends? She found herself gazing at the flat black water, looking for a ripple. Wouldn't it be fun to see something? But it was beginning to snow and she didn't want to have to add slick roads to the challenge of driving in Scotland.

It was trickier than she expected to pull back onto the 'wrong' side of the road. She waited. The snowflakes were big and lovely. Finally, when no other cars were coming, she crept out. She shoved the stick into second gear and finally drove down the road like a regular person.

The snow was beginning to stick, and Melissa's imagination shifted from thoughts of Ness to Christmas. The snow added a sparkling layer of frosting to the hilly countryside and the loch, and she enjoyed the drive, humming Christmas carols along with the radio. The loch grew wider and the snow was falling heavier when she finally spotted a sign: Greenhill House. She was home.

CHAPTER 5

*M*elissa pulled into the driveway. Greenhill House was made of gray stone, with white painted wood windows and a bright, cheery front door painted red. The house was two stories, with pointed peaks around several upstairs windows, some windows lovingly caressed by vines, holly bushes and a stone fence around the outskirts, and the back nestled on the pine tree lined banks of Loch Ness.

Melissa couldn't believe it. It was like something out of a movie. She pulled out her phone and was just about to take another selfie when she noticed a real estate sign in front of the house.

"It's not for sale anymore," Melissa said with a grin.

She tugged on the sign and threw it on the side of the driveway. Then Melissa decided to explore her new property. Around the side of the house, Melissa noticed - and appreciated - a stack of firewood on a rack. She'd need more, but that was a start. Directly behind the house was an ancient-looking stone well, its wooden roof covered in snow.

Intrigued, Melissa walked over to it. It looked like a well she had once purchased for her fairy garden, but this one was real and life-sized. The base was made of a circle of stones, there was a wooden roof and a rope with a bucket. The crank looked old, but as Melissa looked down the well she could see that there was, in fact, water there.

Then a small, iron plaque caught her eye. She dusted off the snow and read:

This sacred well was first discovered in 565. The well soon became known not only for its healing properties but locals also believed a sincere wish made at the well would come true, if one was pure of heart. In 1762 Domhnall MacKenzie came to this well with the wish that his sweetheart, Beitidh Urquhart, would marry him. Upon his proposal she happily consented. They married December 24, 1762 and built a home here that has stayed in the MacKenzie family for generations.

What a wonderful story, Melissa thought. She peered down the well and thought about a young man making a wish for love. She turned back to the house he'd built and appreciated it even more.

"Now it's time to check out the inside!" said Melissa as she hurried back around to the front of the house. She tried the front door. It was locked. She looked under the doormat and spotted a key. She opened the door and went inside.

As she stepped into the wide, spacious foyer, an alarm screamed. Melissa covered her ears as she walked over to a pad of numbers on the wall. Some were dirtier than others. She tried 1234 and the alarm turned off.

"Problem one, solved. You go, girl."

That's when she noticed the drips coming from the ceiling.

"We'll just get a bucket and then call a handyman – handy person – and a little paint. No problem."

She strolled through the kitchen, which had beautiful antique windows. Exposed wood beams and gray stonework gave it a cozy cottage feel. The fridge was probably thirty years old, small and rusted. She opened it and shut it immediately, holding her nose. Yeech!

"Okay, so we'll have to clean that out. Or throw the whole thing out. Immediately."

The adjacent dining room had a wood-burning stove and was stocked with wood. A mouse scurried across the floor.

"Hi there, little fella. We'll be finding you a new home once I get some traps. You can explore the great outdoors. Look at that beautiful loch out there." She opened the side door in hopes it would leave, but it scurried into a hole in the wall.

"Add to list: exterminator. Dry wall repair."

The living room was spacious with huge bay windows and lovely wood floors but had serious 70s vibes. She looked at the orange curtains and zebra striped couch and decided to take down the curtains immediately, which she did. "That's better." Right away it was a huge improvement. Melissa paused to look out at the wooded lot and the loch below, now dusted with snow. Down the hill, on the banks of the loch, Melissa spotted two medium-sized spotted brown deer munching on leaves. Their ears pricked up and they stood very still.

"It's okay, sweetie. We can share this place." The deer looked at her, then relaxed and went back to eating the leaves.

When she returned her gaze to the room she was jolted again at the sight of the horrible couch. "That's just hideous. Adding slipcovers to the list."

She turned the corner and her jaw dropped. It was the coziest, most amazing library she'd ever seen. Actually, she'd never seen a library in a home. This place was stacked floor to ceiling with shelves and already stocked with all kinds of wonderful books. There were antique books, poetry, Shakespeare, a whole wall of Robert Burns books of all different editions, modern mysteries and romances, classics of literature, a foreign language section and history and modern literary fiction and even a Sci-Fi/horror section. The exposed wood, wall of windows and stone fireplace was icing on the cake.

"I'm not going to change a thing," Melissa said, settling into a cozy chair and imagining the roaring fire and some tea at her side. Maybe a dog.

"I'm so glad I didn't sell this place. A few curtains, some slipcovers, a coat of paint and this will be paradise."

She toddled up the stairs. There were three bedrooms, all with gorgeous window views of the loch and trees, but all in need of a little TLC.

"New light fixtures, some new bedspreads. You got this, Melissa."

She was heading down the stairs when she heard police sirens roaring down the street.

She looked out the window just in time to see two police cars pull into her driveway.

She opened the door for them.

"What seems to be the problem, officer?" she said before she realized how stupid and American that was going to sound. The taller officer frowned. Were they even called officers here? Bobbies? No. They looked just like the police at home – dark uniform, hat, shiny badge.

"Breaking and entering, ma'am," said the tall one as he reached into his pocket for handcuffs.

"And trespassing," said the shorter one. As they reached for her arm, Melissa wriggled away.

"Oh, no. This is my place. I'm Melissa Mackenzie. I've inherited this from a long-lost relative," she said. She was sure that would clear everything up. But just in case, she rummaged around in her bag.

"Here's the letter. See?"

They looked at the letter. The shorter police officer looked up first. "So the alarm...?"

"The real estate company that notified me had planned to sell the house and give me the money but I decided I'd rather keep it. It's beautiful, isn't it? Just needs a little TLC?" said Melissa, beaming, despite the fact that there was water actively dripping on her from the ceiling. She stepped aside.

"*Aye*, this was a lovely home at one time. My wife was friends with the owner. Kept to himself. Never took care of it after his wife passed on, God rest his soul."

"See? This is a blessing," said Melissa.

The taller police officer was still suspicious. "How'd you get in?" he asked.

"The key. Under the mat," said Melissa, pointing.

"Might want to change where you keep that," said the tall police officer.

"Right," said Melissa.

'Right' was like 'okay' here, in the UK. Melissa decided maybe she shouldn't say 'right'. Her thoughts were beginning to drift into a long-winded daydream, but the shorter police officer interrupted her digressive thoughts.

"Could we have a copy of that letter? We'd like to look into this further. I had thought it was for sale—" he began before Melissa cut him off.

"Yes, well, the realtors were going to sell it and give me the money—"

"You said that, but—"

"It's fine. I'm sure. But, sure, take a picture if you'd like," she said, realizing she'd have to get out of the habit of interrupting, especially in another country and especially with police officers.

They snapped a picture of the letter, tipped their hats, and let her go. Or at least, didn't arrest her. They were the ones who left.

Melissa took a deep breath and waved as they backed out of the driveway. Then she closed the door and looked around. This was her house. Her mice. Her zebra striped couch. Her dripping ceiling. She twirled around like Julie Andrews in *The Sound of Music*. Mine. It's all mine, she thought.

CHAPTER 6

$\mathcal{M}$elissa gingerly drove the narrow, snow-covered road back to Inverness. She pulled up and parked outside a small, independent hardware store. The front door jingled as she opened it. Christmas music played as Melissa filled a cart with cleaning supplies, shades, curtains, buckets, putty, paint... Everything. She pushed her cart to the front of the store where the shop owner, a cute older man, stood at the register. He had twinkly eyes, not unlike the Jolly Old Elf himself.

"Hi. I'm just moving here from across the pond and I could use some recommendations," said Melissa.

"Welcome. How can I help?" he asked.

"I am looking for so many things. I need some help with construction and repairs to start," she said.

"Fergus Dunbar is the best lad in town for that. He lives over by the lumberyard, and I'll get you his contact information."

"Great."

"What else can I do for you?" asked the man.

"Well, I'm so new here I barely even know where to start..."

The shop owner pulled out a folder full of town pamphlets, maps, organizations, and activities.

"Of course, you'll want to join the Community website, and you'll want to know about the pipe competition going on this week, and the Highland Games celebration, the Christmas *Ceilidh*, and Hogmanay celebrations."

"What's a *ceilidh*?"

"A party with dancing. You'll love it," he said.

"And Hog- Hogman—"

"Hogmanay. That's our biggest holiday of the year. New Year's celebrations."

"Oh, right. Gotcha. Great." said Melissa, feeling a little silly.

Melissa paid and headed for the door, then stopped back.

"Thanks so much, Sir. And I forgot to ask. Is there a place I can buy a lot of firewood?"

"Sandy MacGregor can help you out. Here's his address," he said, handing her a business card.

CHAPTER 7

As Melissa pulled into the MacGregor's driveway, she couldn't help but notice what a perfect cozy Scottish cottage this was – stone and wood, with well-tended landscaping and set against a backdrop of rolling green hills, dotted with about a hundred adorable little sheep. A man in the distance in a gray sweater and dark pants surveyed the sheep. Outside, a brawny man in a kilt was chopping wood. Melissa stepped out of the car, holding a thermal mug of coffee, and admiring the strong arms of the lumberjack at work. She slammed the door shut and the brawny kilt man turned. It was Colin MacGregor.

Melissa dropped her coffee to the ground. Colin wiped his brow.

"Ms. Mackenzie. How can I help you?" he asked. She couldn't take her eyes off of him. Who would've known that charming man in tweed from the airport secretly looked like he'd just stepped out of a Scottish lumberjack calendar.

"I'm so sorry. I had no idea. The man at the hardware store sent me here for firewood..." Melissa stumbled, trying to avert her eyes.

"Of course. How's Mr. Douglas doing?"

"Very friendly," she managed, trying to sound cool.

He laid down his axe.

"So you need some firewood?" he asked.

"Uh, yeah. Yes. Please."

"It's late in the season. Winters here gets quite brisk," he said, putting on a plaid flannel.

Melissa pulled her sweater over her shoulders.

"Okay. How does it work?" she asked.

"We deliver. I can bring it by this afternoon, if that suits you," he said.

"You? I thought you were here on holiday," she asked.

"This is a crofter's holiday. No rest for the wicked," he smiled.

Melissa was desperate to shift her gaze from his still unbuttoned shirt, so she looked out into the hills behind their home.

"I love all the sheep. What's that man doing out there? Is he a shepherd?"

"That's my da. Come. You'll have to see this."

Melissa followed him behind the house toward the sheep-filled hills.

The man walked down the hill to meet them. He

was an older man, in his 70s, but not frail. He had gray hair, a tweed cap and was the spitting image of his son – if his son had remained in Scotland. He extended his hand.

"Alexander MacGregor. Pleasure to meet you. Please call me Sandy."

"Pleasure to meet you. I'm Melissa Mackenzie," she responded.

"An American. Colin, you didn't tell me—" he began, a twinkle in his eye.

"Oh, no. It's just… we're just—" Melissa fumbled.

"We met at the airport and, by coincidence, Melissa has inherited the old Mackenzie place, Greenhill House," said Colin.

"Good on you. Lovely place, that. Right on the loch, aye?"

"Yes. You know, Colin, it's strange. I stopped by the real estate office twice and no one's there. But I have the key and the letter, so everything was just fine when the police—"

"The police?"

"Oh, yeah. Well, they stopped by because I set off some alarms," said Melissa, feeling a little silly.

"I'll continue to look into the matter for you," he said.

"Oh, well, thanks, Colin. You don't have to..." but Melissa couldn't finish speaking because the world's most adorable border collie had trotted up to Alexander. "What a great dog."

"Who's a good dog? What a good dog. Doggie, doggie..."

"He's a work dog," said Alexander. "Let me show you." Alexander whistled and the dog sprang into action. The dog raced up the hill as if his life depended on it. Alexander whistled a different pattern, and the dog turned toward the sheep. He whistled a new pattern, and the dog somehow was getting the sheep to all turn. The sheep all began walking down the hill.

"Amazing!" said Melissa.

"That's my da," Colin nodded.

"And the dog knows just how to—"

"Watch," said Colin, pointing.

"Sit!" shouted Alexander. Even though the dog was far away, it heard his master's voice and sat. The sheep stood still.

"Left or right?" Alexander asked Melissa.

"Right?"

He tweeted the whistle and the dog steered all the sheep to the right, and down the hill.

The dog then sat and the sheep stood still.

"That's amazing! Wow! Bravo!" Melissa applauded through her muffled red mittens.

"Come. Let's get your firewood sorted out," said Colin. They walked back toward the house, passing a barn.

"That reminds me, I was thinking of getting a dog myself. You know, to put the house in its name so Dave couldn't get it."

Colin grinned. "Come with me," he said, beckoning.

And when a handsome man in a kilt beckons, you follow…

In the warm barn, amid the hay and gear, there was a small stall. Colin opened the door to reveal a mother and six adorable border collie puppies.

"Oh my gosh. They're adorable."

"Da says they're just the right age for new homes. Which one do you want?"

A little black and white puppy had crawled up on Melissa's leg and was licking her face.

"Hello. Are you my dog? Are you? I love you, too. I do. Yes. Yes, I do. You wanna come live with me?"

"I think we have a winner," said Colin.

"How does it work? Do I need to submit adoption papers? How much does it cost?"

"Rubbish. Consider it a gift. Welcome to Scotland," said Colin with a smile.

Melissa teared up. "Oh, thank you. That's the nicest thing ever."

She hugged Colin and then became suddenly aware that he was a hunk of muscular, kilted, brawny… She backed up and so did he.

"Er, no worries. My pleasure, Ms. Mackenzie," he said.

"Thank you, Mr. MacGregor. "

He handed her the puppy, which she immediately cuddled, making it difficult to hold the bag of puppy food he also gave her.

"This will get you started until you can get to a pet supply store. I'll be over this afternoon with the kindling."

"Ok, see you then." Melissa took the frisky little puppy into the back of her car.

CHAPTER 8

*A*s Melissa gripped the steering wheel and concentrated on driving on the other side of the road, the little puppy kept jumping into the front seat near the gear shift.

"Baby, I really have to concentrate here." She looked down at the puppy and then looked up to see a round-about.

She swerved into the wrong lane and nearly crashed into a car. She took a deep breath, finished the round-about and stopped at a pet supply store.

Melissa carried the puppy inside with her. It kept licking her face. She spotted a clerk.

"What a sweet puppy," said the clerk. "Puppy supplies?"

"How'd you guess?" smiled Melissa.

"Follow me."

Melissa followed the clerk and filled a cart with food and toys. Then they stopped in front of the cages.

"I don't want a cage."

"Some people just find it's nice for the little ones to have a place to sleep while they're, uh... training."

"Oh my gosh. It's been so long since I've had a dog. I'm a cat person, usually, but after my cat died my husband - ex-husband - didn't want a new one. Where do I get a bag of litter?"

"Oh, no. I meant paper training. Dogs don't use—"

"Oh. Of course. I guess I need to learn how to train a dog. Do you know any good trainers?"

"Alexander MacGregor's the best in town. He lives at—"

Melissa nodded. "That's where I got this little guy."

"He does a show at the Christmas Highland Games every year. Are you coming?"

"Sounds like fun. I haven't heard of it," said Melissa.

"Here's a brochure. There's Highland dancing, all the regular games, you know, the caber toss, the hammer throw, then you've got the sheep dog herding shows, the bake-off."

"Bake off? Maybe I could do that," said Melissa.

"Toss your hat in the ring. It's a lot of fun," said the clerk.

"Great. Thanks. I'm Melissa, by the way. Melissa Mackenzie," she said, extending her hand.

"Related to Gerald Mackenzie?"

"Hmmm. I don't think so? I just inherited Stuart Mackenzie's house," said Melissa, feeling a bit awkward.

"Lovely. Nice to meet you," said the clerk.

BACK AT HER home Melissa carried the supplies out of the car as her happy little scampering puppy followed.

"You need a name. What should we call you? Angus? Bobby Burns? Alba? Kenzie?"

She opened the front door and the puppy followed her inside. She set out a bowl of food and water, which the puppy munched on. She petted him and looked out the windows at the peaceful views of the dark waters of Loch Ness.

"Good dog," she said, patting him on the head.

Melissa went to the fridge. Empty.

"Drat. I keep forgetting to get some groceries."

CHAPTER 9

The car was full of groceries but it was snowing and Melissa's stomach was growling. She spotted a little sandwich café on the outskirts of town and turned into the car park.

"Just one," Melissa told the hostess, who seated her in a cozy spot by the window.

Melissa looked at all the unfamiliar items on the menu. "Cockamaimie soup? Cootie pudding? No, thanks," said Melissa with a chuckle.

"Cock-a-leekie. Chicken soup with leeks. And the pudding is called Clootie. It gets its name from the cloth it's baked in. If you haven't tried it, I'll get you a sample. Will you be having tea with that?" said the waitress.

Melissa flushed with embarrassment. She always blurted out her thoughts. 'No filter' is what Dave had said.

"She'll have the pudding with tea and the cock-a-leekie. And also a cup of cullen skink. On me," said a woman about Melissa's age.

"Straightaway," said the waitress.

The woman smiled. "If you're having trouble with the menu, you must have come from away," she said.

"Yes. I'm from Boston," said Melissa. "I'm so sorry you heard me. I don't mean to be an ugly American."

"No worries. I'm Lindsay," she said.

"Melissa. Nice to meet you."

"Likewise." Lindsay gestured to the empty chair beside her. "May I?"

"Please."

"Are you here on holiday?"

"Well, I'm going to live here. I inherited a home and my marriage ... well. I decided I should try something new."

"Wonderful. We have loads of good adventures here. Do you like hill walking? Or with the holidays coming, you might enjoy the town Christmas baking competition."

"That sounds like fun," said Melissa.

"We start this Saturday. Here's the address." Lindsay handed her a card.

The waitress returned with two different kinds of soup.

"This one is Cullen skink. This is what the Scots brought to New England, and then you Americans used it as the basis for your New England Clam Chowder."

Melissa tried a taste. "It's so smoky. I love it."

Lindsay grinned. "The smoke can be an acquired taste."

"But the rest is so much like clam chowder."

Melissa tried the cock-a-leekie soup. "This is good, too."

"Basically standard chicken soup with a Scottish slant, the leeks."

"What's this clootie pudding thing, then?"

"So pudding is always dessert, but not necessarily what those of you from across the pond think of as pudding. We have clootie dumplings and clootie pudding. They're basically the same thing. Spiced pudding wrapped in cloth – that's the clootie – and simmered in water."

Melissa took a taste. "Oh. That reminds me of something. Yes, that's wonderful. Maybe something old fashioned from Boston. Not quite Indian pudding. Not quite bread pudding. But something."

They sat and enjoyed their tea.

"Thanks for sitting here. I don't know anyone in town yet. I mean, just the shop keepers and such. Literally, that's all."

"Well, come to the baking competition this weekend and then I'll introduce you around."

"Nice to meet you."

"See you soon!" Lindsay waved as she headed to her car.

CHAPTER 10

Melissa pulled into her snow-covered driveway to find another FOR SALE sign in the yard. She parked the car and immediately went over to the sign and plucked it out of the yard and into the trash bin just as Colin arrived with his truck.

Colin, now in jeans and a flannel shirt, got out of his truck and began to unload the firewood.

As Melissa opened the front door her little dog jumped out and scampered behind her.

"He's definitely feeling at home," said Colin.

"Yes. I've got to get him a name."

"Or maybe a friend. Or some sheep. He'll want something to herd soon enough," said Colin.

"You're right. I've heard that about border collies. Maybe I will." Melissa began carrying groceries into the house.

"So have you made an offer on the house? Let me

know if you need any legal help," said Colin as he picked up a bag of dog food to help her.

"An offer? No, I'm not taking offers, I've decided not to sell it. I'm going to fix it up."

"Did you buy it from the bank?" asked Colin.

"No, I inherited it. Remember?" Melissa was juggling groceries and the front door, so Colin opened it for her, and followed her into the house. He dodged the drip, which was slowing, and looked around.

"Lovely. Really. Loads of possibilities," he said.

"Just a little paint here, fix a leak there..."

"Where would you like this?" asked Colin, nodding to his bag of groceries.

"I guess the kitchen?"

He followed her into the kitchen and was awestruck by the wall of windows overlooking the loch. He stood gazing out at the dark water and the hills on the other side of the narrow loch.

"Just takes your breath away," he said.

"It really does, doesn't it?" Melissa realized she kind of meant him and looked away. He did as well.

"Where would you like me to unload - some by the fire and some in the stack by the side of the house?"

"That would be wonderful. On both counts," said Melissa.

Colin went back outside and began to haul the firewood. He stacked it by the wood-burning stove in the kitchen.

"You should really meet my sister. She's in charge of a lot of the Christmas festival, so she can introduce you to a lot of people in town. I'll be headed back to the States after Hogmanay, so..."

"That would be great," said Melissa.

"Why don't you come to dinner tonight? I'll introduce you."

"That would be gre--lovely. What time?" She hoped she didn't sound too American, trying to add in words like 'lovely' for the benefit of the Scot.

"How about half six?"

"I'll be there," said Melissa.

"Lovely," said Colin. He wasn't talking about her, but she flushed anyway.

CHAPTER 11

*M*elissa drove back to the MacGregor farmhouse – in the twilight, the home looked like a perfect cozy dream. It was all lit up in sparkling white lights and greenery. Icicle lights hung from the roof and the shrubs were covered in white light netting. White lights and red ornaments dotted the large pine tree in front of the house and a large evergreen wreath hung on the red front door. Melissa knocked on the brass door knocker. Colin opened the door.

"Hello!" Melissa handed him a bottle of wine.

Alexander "Sandy" MacGregor came up behind Colin and accepted it. "Colin, so nice to have your girl-friend over for dinner," said Sandy with a grin.

"Oh, I'm here to meet—" began Melissa.

"I just wanted Melissa to meet more people in town, so I thought I'd introduce her to Lindsay."

Sandy nodded, not believing this story in the slightest. As they walked toward the living room, Melissa recognized the woman she'd met at the cafe.

"Lindsay!"

"Melissa! Good to see you," Lindsay said.

"I didn't know you were a MacGregor," said Melissa, while Colin looked confused and Sandy looked amused.

"You already know each other?" asked Colin.

"We met at the café in town," said Melissa.

Lindsay brought out bowls of Cullen skink.

Colin began to explain, "You'll love this. It's a bit like clam chowder like you have in Boston, but this is the original. Smokey and—"

"She's already had it." said Lindsay. "You didn't think your sister wouldn't teach a newcomer about Cullen skink in this *dreich*."

Colin grinned.

"Who in this town don't you know?" asked Colin. "I thought you didn't know anyone yet?"

"I don't know anyone. Just you, your dad, Lindsay, the people at the hardware store, the people at the pet store, the people at the grocery store—"

They laughed.

"Once you get involved in the Christmas Festival, you'll know the whole town. And you'll meet the rest when you walk the dog. Does he have a name yet?"

"I was thinking maybe Nick, like St. Nick?"

"Good name," said Lindsay.

Lindsay passed a plate of oat cakes and they ate their soup and talked and chatted.

While they ate, the snow began falling more intensely.

"We might have to get out the toboggan," said Lindsay, with a twinkle in her eye.

"I'm too old for that," said Colin.

"If I'm able to do it, you can do it," said Sandy.

Melissa watched the family dynamics and enjoyed their banter. "Sounds like fun."

They finished their meal and Melissa helped Colin and Lindsay with the dishes while Sandy went out to do some chores.

Christmas lights twinkled in the trees and around the yard as the snow fell. It was quiet, except for the sounds of the sheep in the hills.

"Who's first? Melissa and Colin?" asked Sandy as he emerged from the barn with a shiny red toboggan.

"What about the sheep?"

"They'll move out of the way," said Lindsay.

Melissa wasn't reassured.

Colin and Melissa climbed the steep snow-covered hill, passing the bah-ing sheep, and set up the toboggan.

"Ready?"

"This is a bigger hill than it looks," said Melissa, looking down.

"Quite," said Colin.

Alexander gave them a shove and they were off. Melissa clutched Colin as they leaned left and right in attempt to steer away from the sheep. But they were barreling straight toward them. Melissa screamed and the sheep, fortunately, scuttled out of the way just in the nick of time. They were still only half-way down the hill when they hit a rock and went flying, landing in a heap almost on top of each other. Melissa was covered in snow. Colin gently helped her brush it off. She looked beautiful in the moonlight with the snow in her hair. Colin looked as if he were about to say something, then thought better of it.

"Right. Let me help you up?" he offered his hand. There was an electricity between them they both noticed. Alexander noticed as well, but he grabbed the toboggan.

"Our turn now. You hold the chocolate," said Sandy.

Sandy and his daughter climbed the hill and soon come screaming down the hill.

BACK AT THE MACGREGOR HOME, Melissa warmed her hands by the fire as Sandy opened what looked to be a special bottle of Scotch whisky.

"How about a wee dram to warm us up?" he asked, pouring everyone a glass before they could protest.

Colin raised his glass. "To new adventures," he said.

Sandy grinned and looked at Colin and Melissa.

"To new adventures."

"Aye."

"*Slàinte.*"

"Say it again?" Melissa asked.

"Slant-yuh. Or maybe Slanch-yuh."

"*Slàinte,*" Melissa tried it out.

"*Slàinte mhath,*" said Lindsay.

"Now what's that one?" asked Melissa.

"It's the response. It means, 'and to you as well' or 'good health to you as well,'" explained Colin.

"It's written here on this little framed wall sign Da has," said Lindsay.

"But wow, you sure don't spell it the way you say it."

"That's Gaelic for you."

"And you pronounce Gaelic like we'd say GAH-lick in Boston. You know, the thing that keeps vampires away," said Melissa. "I always thought it was GAY-lick."

"That's Irish Gaelic. This is Scots Gaelic," said Sandy. And Melissa knew enough to know they were very different.

"Well, *Slàinte Mhath* to you as well," she said. They all laughed. "That's like asking for something with *au juice* sauce, right? Redundant?"

"*Dinnae fash yerself,*" said Lindsay, her Scots accent emerging with the drink. Colin's eyes were dancing until they locked eyes and he looked away and sipped his scotch.

"THANK you so much for inviting me," said Melissa.

"Our pleasure," said Colin.

"So you'll come over Friday and we'll bake?" asked Lindsay.

"Or you could come over to my new place. I could

definitely use another set of eyes on it for decorating ideas."

"That would be lovely. Then Saturday the Highland Games kick off the festival."

"And the pipe band competition," added Sandy.

"Of course," said Lindsay.

Colin's cell rang. He looked troubled. "Excuse me. I have to take this. It's - er, a client."

Melissa frowned as Colin walked into another room. Alexander frowned as well.

"I'm sorry about that, Melissa. Since he's moved to the States, he's obsessed with work. A regular Yank - er, I mean..."

"It's okay. He's got a tough client," she said.

"Oh? He's told you of his work?"

"That's how we met. He, uh, represents my husband. Or soon to be ex-husband."

There was a long pause and an awkward silence.

"Lindsay, could you point me in the direction of the powder room? Or the loo?" asked Melissa.

"Just down the hall and to the right," Lindsay said quickly.

Melissa followed Lindsay's directions, leaving Alexander and Lindsay alone while Colin spoke in hushed tones into the phone. Though she couldn't hear Colin, she could hear Alexander and Lindsay loud and clear.

"So, is Colin... the other man?" Melissa heard Sandy ask Lindsay.

"Da. Melissa and Colin are not involved. They're

just friends. They met at the airport and it was just coincidence that they both ended up in this town."

Alexander sounded truly surprised. "I thought he was just saying that. I was going to invite Caitlin Munro over but he'd told me he'd met someone."

Melissa's ears perked up.

"Oh, yeah. There's a lawyer he's been dating. She's spending the holidays with her family."

"Oh. I see. So he does have someone?"

"Yes," said Lindsay.

Melissa took a deep breath and stepped back into the hallway.

"I liked Melissa," said Sandy.

"I like her, too," said Lindsay with a grin.

Melissa returned. She couldn't see a reason to pretend she hadn't overhead, so she chimed in with the conversation.

"And I like you guys. It was a pleasure, really. I think I'd better get home and see how the little munchkin is doing," she said.

"Have you decided on a name yet?"

"I was thinking Nick. Or Snowball. Or Belle. Something Christmassy…"

"Haggis," said Sandy.

"Jingles. Maybe Jingles."

"It has a nice ring to it," said Lindsay.

"I see what you did there," said Melissa. "Thanks again. I really should head back."

"I apologize for Colin…" said Sandy.

"That's okay, really. Work beckons."

"Are you quite all right to drive?"

"Yes, I'm fine. Thank you." She'd only had a sip. Scotch must be an acquired taste, she thought. She had yet to acquire it.

Light snow was falling as Melissa walked to her car. She loved the sound of her boots crunching in the snow, and was grateful that it was such light snow she could brush it off of the windshield with her arm.

"Melissa."

Melissa turned to find Colin running down the driveway to catch up with her.

"Yes?"

"I, uh. Thank you for coming. This was fun. I'm glad you met Lindsay. Or already had," he said.

"Yeah, thank you. It was fun," said Melissa.

"Your husband... I mean, Dave..."

"Yes?"

"You have a good lawyer? Do you need a recommendation?" Colin looked concerned.

Melissa bit her lip. "I have a lawyer. I hope he's good," she said.

"Me too."

CHAPTER 12

Melissa sang Christmas love songs along with the radio until the Ramones singing "Christmas (Baby Please Come Home)" made her tear up. She switched to another channel and settled on "Sleigh Ride."

When she pulled into her driveway she noticed how very dark it was. "I've gotta get some lights out here."

She opened her notes app and added 'lights' to the long list of to-dos. She opened the door and let the puppy outside.

"I'm going to call you Jingles," she said as she cuddled him. He licked her face again and wagged his fluffy little tail. "We'll have to get you some bells for your collar."

He followed her into the kitchen, where she opened her now fully-stocked fridge. She poured a glass of local eggnog, added nutmeg, and sat by the fire. Jingles sat at her feet. Melissa looked at the fire, her new dog and the snow outside and smiled.

CHAPTER 13

The gingerbread house competition was a much bigger event than Melissa could have imagined. Dozens of teams sat at tables set up with baking materials: bowls of candy, sprinkles, frostings. Judges, dressed as Santa and Mrs. Claus, milled about giving directions, looking at the timer, and munching on cookies.

Melissa and Lindsay were busy building a majestic gingerbread model of Greenhill House. They had little turrets covered in frosting, a spun sugar model of the Loch shimmered behind the home, powdered sugar snow dusted the roof, the grounds and the sugary trees. Little gingerbread men stood in the back carrying a gingerbread toboggan.

"What else do we need?" asked Lindsay.

"Santa," said Melissa.

They rolled the dough. Lindsay selected a Santa cutter and Melissa found a little tiny dog cookie cutter.

They cut them out and popped the cookies into the oven.

"Fifteen minutes. Fifteen minutes," called the judge, an older woman in a white Mrs. Claus wig, round glasses and a red apron.

Melissa peeked into the oven. "We've got to let them set, too," said Melissa.

Other teams had created elaborate castles, cozy villages, fairy glen scenes, and more. The timer dinged. Melissa pulled out the cookies.

"They've got to cool. What can we do while we wait?" asked Lindsay.

They began adding red and green candies and spreading white frosting snow around the scene. When they were cool Melissa frosted them like a pro. They arranged the Santa and sleigh on top of the house and used candy as presents.

"Ten... nine... eight..." called the judge.

Melissa frantically set the dog into the sleigh and put a present in his mouth. At the last second, she remembered she's made a Nessie, and she put it into the loch behind the house with a little red bow around its neck. Lindsay put a tiny little candy camera in the hands of the gingerbread people on the banks of the Loch.

"Five... Four... three...two... one... Hands off."

Melissa and Lindsay raised their hands, done. The judges walked around remarking on each gingerbread project. When the woman in the Mrs. Claus outfit arrived, Melissa offered her a gingerbread person.

"What have we here?" she asked, munching on a cookie.

"This is my new home, Greenhill House, on the banks of Loch Ness," said Melissa.

"As you can see, we have Santa landing his sleigh on top of the house and Melissa's little dog, Jingles, has a present."

"And in the back, here, we have a Nessie sighting. And the little gingerbread people see both Nessie and Santa - they're not sure which one to take the picture of," Melissa said.

The judge wrinkled her nose. "You take the picture of Santa," she said, and walked away.

Melissa looked crestfallen. "Too much?"

"Don't worry about it. It's adorable," said Lindsay.

The judge tapped a microphone. "And the winner is: Allison MacDonald, with her replica of Inverness castle as Santa's workshop."

Melissa grabbed a gingerbread Christmas tree from their submission and ate it.

Lindsay giggled. "Let's get out of here."

MELISSA AND LINDSAY walked down High Street in downtown Inverness carrying shopping bags. Bagpipes played in the distance as happy shoppers filled with Christmas cheer went from one store to the next. They stopped to listen as carolers sang "Ding Dong Merrily on High." Lindsay and Melissa clapped for the carolers and continued walking along the shops.

"Are you excited for the Highland games?" asked Lindsay.

"What are they, exactly?" asked Melissa as she accepted a candy cane from a shopkeeper.

"Just you wait. Do you have a tartan sash?" asked Lindsay.

"A what?" asked Melissa.

Lindsay took her by the arm into a tartan shop. The shopkeeper, dressed in a tartan skirt and wool sweater with what Melissa would soon learn was a tartan sash, greeted them.

"In Scotland if you go to a formal event, like a wedding, most of the men will be in their dress kilts. Women have some leeway. I like to wear a simple black dress with a tartan sash and maybe matching tartan shoes. Some people go all out and wear a full tartan dress," Lindsay explained, showing Melissa a red and green plaid tartan dress.

"I love it," said Melissa, until she looked at the price and blinked.

"That's why I wear a tartan sash. Come on, they're over here," said Lindsay.

They looked at sashes of all kinds of tartan – red Royal Stewart, blue and green Gordon, purple Scotland Forever, yellow MacLeod, yellow red and green Buchanan…

"So you'd wear Mackenzie, right? Is that your father's name or your--"

"It's my father's name," said Melissa as she browsed through the racks "In fact, here it is." Melissa held up a blue and green plaid sash with white and red stripes.

"Lovely," said Lindsay.

"What else do I need?"

"Do you want the shoes?" asked Lindsay.

Melissa looked at the shoes on display. They were pricey as well. She shook her head.

"No, I think I'm good," she said. She paused at the clan pins. She spotted a Mackenzie pin and read the motto.

"*Luceo Non Uro* - 'I shine, not burn.' I like it."

"It's a good motto," agreed Lindsay.

Melissa took the pin and sash to the cash register. Then she looked back at the shoes. Christmas present to myself, she thought, and set them on the counter along with the rest. "So do I wear all this to the games?"

"Oh, no. You can just wear a sweater and jeans. But some people do like a splash of tartan, so you can wear the sash if you want. I'll pick you up tomorrow morning?"

"Great. Thanks, Lindsay."

CHAPTER 14

*M*elissa stepped out of her car and took in the scene. Tents dotted the frost-covered countryside. Some sold merchandise - tartan sashes, kilts, clan motto T-shirts, etc. and others served as a temporary headquarters for each clan. Burly men in kilts - and Santa hats - trudged toward a field where a caber toss was in session. Pipe bands milled about, practicing, twirling drumsticks and adjusting their kilts. Food trucks sold all kinds of goodies from haggis to shortbread to deep-fried Mars bars, beer and whisky. A little kiddie train chugged through the whole area, taking kids through a Santa Workshop Wonderland filled with little mechanical elves, reindeer, and Santa and Mrs. Claus.

Mr. MacGregor spotted her and walked over. "Good to have you here, Ms. Mackenzie. And I see you've got your tartan."

Melissa self-consciously adjusted her Mackenzie tartan sash. "Yes. And I see you're in your kilt."

"I never miss an opportunity. We're doing another border collie demonstration on the main field at two. Stop by."

"I will. And by the way, I told Jingles – that's what I named him – to sit and he did."

"Of course he did."

"But he's so young."

"He's a MacGregor border collie. He knows 'sit', 'stay' and 'down' as well as some of my training whistles." He patted her on the shoulder and greeted another friend.

The sound of bagpipes drew Melissa over to a tent where teenage girls dressed in colorful pleated skirts and argyle socks were dancing a traditional Scottish dance over swords.

"If the soldiers could dance without touching the sword, they'd have success in battle, but if a soldier's foot touched the sword, it meant disaster," explained a woman with a microphone. "Some believe the tradition began with Malcom III, who danced over his dead enemy's corpse with his sword on the ground beside the body."

Melissa shuddered and continued on along through the shops, buying a beautiful wreath and other decorations for her new house.

She arrived at the pipe band competition and was startled to see Colin dressed to the nines in his kilt with a snare drum strapped to his waist.

"Is there anything you can't do?" she asked with a grin.

The band began to form lines.

"Off we go." Colin waved a drum stick as he joined the ranks of the rest of the pipe band. Melissa waved and the band began marching. They played a lot of familiar tunes and quite a few that Melissa didn't know. Lindsay caught up with her.

"Hey. How's it going?" asked Lindsay.

"This is so amazing."

"Right?"

"You know, I think I know this song but I have no idea what it's called," said Melissa.

"That's 'Scotland the Brave'," she said.

"Ah. I knew I'd heard it a lot. Do you know the words?"

"I know one verse. My da would be disappointed I don't know the whole thing. Here it comes around...

High in the misty Highlands,
Out by the purple islands,
Brave are the hearts that beat
Beneath Scottish skies.
Wild are the winds to meet you,
Staunch are the friends that greet you,
Kind as the love that shines
From fair maidens' eyes."

.   .   .

"That's beautiful," said Melissa. "Wow, I'm tearing up or something." She laughed, trying to blink back the tears.

"Let's go see another strength competition."

Men and women alike competed in the stone lifting competition. They all wore utility kilts and clan t-shirts. The women were first. Melissa watched in awe as they bent down, lifted with their knees and hoisted the giant stones over the mark. The crowd cheered, and the first lifter strutted around in her kilt. Now the next one approached the stone.

"Have you ever done this?" asked Melissa.

"Ach, no. Not me. But it's open to anyone. Did you want to—"

"Absolutely not. I'll stick to the baking. Maybe there's a shortbread eating competition?"

"Have you ever had a deep-fried Mars bar?" asked Lindsay.

Before Melissa could ask any questions, Lindsay had steered her into a long line outside a food truck.

"So you really think you're all set to just live here?" asked Lindsay. "What about friends and family from home?'

Melissa thought about it. "You know, a lot of them were friends I had from knowing Dave. I've spent so much time in a relationship I forgot to find out who I am. I think this is a good place to do that."

"I'm sorry. I didn't mean to bring up a sore subject."

"Not at all. It's just something I think about a lot lately."

They moved up in line.

"I wish my brother would move back home."

Melissa didn't know what to say to that. "Maybe he enjoys a new life there the way I enjoy my new life here?"

"Maybe. But I can't help but feel like he's trying to escape."

"We all need some kind of escape sometimes."

The queue behind them had grown to about twenty people. Melissa and Lindsay were next. The food truck was painted blue and white, like the St. Andrew's flag, with a chalkboard menu and a Highland cow on it. Their offerings, per the menu, were deep fried Mars bars, or deep fried Mars bars with ice cream. And Irn Bru.

"Two deep fried Mars bars," said Lindsay, and she paid.

"Thanks."

The clerk handed Melissa a piping hot, lightly fried, ooey, gooey chocolate and caramel sensation.

"Wow."

"Right?"

"We'd better find a table."

They walked over to a nearby tent with tables.

"Do I use a fork or a spoon or my hands or…"

"Just pick it up like you'd eat the candy bar and … down the hatch."

Melissa picked up her deep-fried Mars bar. "It's so warm." She took a bite. "Wow. Someone really knew what they were doing when they invented this."

"It was a man called John Davie, who ran a chippie

in Stonehaven," said Lindsay.

"Well, here's to John Davie for taking a break from frying that healthy stuff and giving us warm, gooey chocolate."

They enjoyed their Mars bars in silence, and in the process, Melissa spilled chocolate on her shirt and her face. "Can't take me anywhere," she joked.

Colin, still in uniform but away from the band, came over to chat.

"So what do you think of the Highland games?"

He'd caught Melissa with her mouth full. She nodded, gestured and quickly tried to swallow.

"Mmmph. Mmmph, mmmph," she said, gesturing in a way that she hoped meant she was enjoying herself.

A tall woman with flowing curls of long red hair tapped Colin on the shoulder.

"Colin MacGregor!" she said.

Colin turned and looked shocked. "Fiona. What brings you here?"

"I heard you were in town, and here you are dressed to the nines in your kilt. Did I miss the pipe band?"

"Aye, just the now, but we'll be back on again in a wee bit," said Colin.

Melissa noticed he had slipped into Scots. She still had a smudge of chocolate on her face. Lindsay gestured with her napkin and Melissa quickly wiped her face.

Melissa extended her hand. "I'm Melissa. Nice to

meet you," she said, hoping the chocolate was gone and she had some form of dignity left.

"Oh. An American. I had thought you must be Colin's aunt," Fiona said.

Melissa's eyes narrowed a bit and Colin covered.

"She does look a wee bit like Catroina, but ... she's certainly much younger—"

"We met at the airport," explained Melissa.

Fiona raised her eyebrows.

"I'm ... uh..." said Colin, flustered.

"He's my husband's divorce lawyer," explained Melissa.

"Oh. I see. So are you two...?" Fiona left the question in the air.

Colin and Melissa looked at each other.

"We're friends," said Melissa.

"Lovely," said Fiona. "Colin and I go way back, don't we? We've known each other for donkey's years, as your da would say." Colin looked a little awkward as Fiona wrapped her arm around his shoulders.

Melissa felt her face flush and she knew she needed to escape. "Great meeting you. I'll be heading back to my new house, then. Thanks for the legal advice, Colin," she said. Melissa quickly blended into the crowd before Colin could say much of anything.

CHAPTER 15

*L*andscape workers were busy around the house cutting down dead branches. Inside painters and drywall workers scurried around the home, avoiding the carpet layers. There was a lot to do, and they were moving quickly, but Melissa was getting overwhelmed with the chaos. Finally when they brought out the chainsaws to cut down trees outside, Melissa had to retreat upstairs.

Melissa was sitting in her bedroom, trying to center herself when her phone rang. "Hello?"

"Melissa. I have the final papers but I don't know where to send them." It was Dave. She hadn't quite forgotten about him, but she almost had. That's progress, she thought.

"Colin didn't give you my address?" she asked.

"Colin who?" said Dave.

"Your lawyer..."

"How would my lawyer have your address?" asked

Dave in that tone she was glad to have nearly forgotten. Melissa bit her lip.

"Right. Okay. So it's Greenhill House, 18 Victoria Way, Inverness IV1 1LG, United Kingdom."

"United Kingdom?"

"Yes. I've inher—I'm living in Scotland."

"What?"

"Yes. I've moved to Scotland. Feel free to send the divorce pages by post, but it might be faster to fax or email them."

"By post...?"

"Ta-ta, Dave. *Dinnae fash yerself.* I'll be happy to sign your papers. And a Happy Christmas to you." Melissa hung up and grinned.

She went downstairs. The workers were cleaning up for the day. They'd put up new drywall where the leak had been and had painted the whole first floor. It looked clean and new.

"Time to start decorating," said Melissa with a grin.

She placed her new wreath from the Highland Games on the front door and then looked around, making a list of what to buy.

IN A DOWNTOWN CHRISTMAS shop Melissa bought an inexpensive box of ornaments, a Christmas tree stand, candles and lights.

At a farm on the outskirts of town Melissa picked out a tree and a young man tied it to her car.

She played Christmas songs on the radio as she drove merrily down the now familiar road along the loch to her home. When she pulled into her driveway, the real estate sign was up again. Was someone playing a prank on her?

Once again she hoisted the sign out of the snowy yard and into the dustbin. "They must have an awful lot of these signs," Melissa said.

Melissa cut the ropes from the tree and dragged it down from the car, then did her best to drag it into the house. It was slow-going, and she left a trail of pine needles in the snow behind her, but she managed to get it inside the house and into the stand she'd bought. Fortunately, the workers had left a giant broom, so she swept them out toward the door easily. As she swept, a car pulled up. Lindsay got out of the car.

"I brought some mulled wine and some extra ornaments. Do you need any help decorating?"

"I was just about to start. You're a lifesaver."

Melissa put on some Christmas music and they began to hang the ornaments.

"Thanks so much, Lindsay. I just got a box of these little glass ornaments. All my other ones are back at the house. I don't know why I didn't think to bring them."

"You were packing for an international flight, not decorating for Christmas."

"You're right."

Melissa looked at some cute little painted reindeer made out of clothespins. "These are adorable."

Lindsay flushed. "We made those in school a long time ago."

"But they're special family heirlooms," Melissa protested.

"We made a lot of ornaments over the years. Don't worry. There's more where these came from. And this way it helps the tree feel more homey."

"Definitely." Melissa stood back and surveyed their work.

"It looks great," said Lindsay. "Wow, look at the walls. This place is really coming along."

"They're doing a great job. I'm so excited."

They plunked down in the chairs.

"I can get the eggnog," said Lindsay.

"I wish we had some cookies to go with it."

"Have you bought any cookie sheets or a mixer?"

"Not yet," said Melissa, beginning to feel over-whelmed at all the things she needed to get. "Do you know of a second-hand store where I could get some?"

"Mine are in the car. Just borrow mine. Let's make some cookies."

Melissa and Lindsay unloaded a giant red Kitchen-Aid mixer, cookie sheets, and a big box of cookie cutters. Lindsay held something behind her back.

"Left or right?" she asked.

"Right?" guessed Melissa.

Lindsay revealed two adorable red and green plaid aprons. The one on the right had more red, the one on the left had more green.

They put on their aprons and began to mix cookie dough.

"So. That Fiona...what a knock out. What's the story there?" Melissa tried to sound nonchalant.

"Oh. Well. She and Colin used to date," said Lindsay.

Melissa nodded and dug a scoop into the dough and plunked it on the cookie sheet.

"And they broke up..."

"Yeah. When he moved to the states. She couldn't get a visa," said Lindsay.

"Ah. And so now he's coming back for her?" Melissa tried to keep her voice light.

Lindsay grimaced. "No. I sure hope not. No, he's here for Da. I'm not sure you know, but he's got so much joint pain and arthritis now he can barely run the dogs, let alone the croft," said Lindsay.

"Oh. I didn't know that. I'm so sorry. He always seems in good spirits."

"Yeah, he does. I know he wishes Colin would stay and run the croft, but Colin loves his life in America. He loves the big city. Being a lawyer."

Melissa put the last cookie on the tray and put them in the oven. "More?"

"Definitely."

Melissa poured another glass of wine for each of them and rolled out more dough.

"So. What's he going to do? I mean, if his girlfriend is here and his dad needs him."

"I get the idea he's had a change of heart," Lindsay said.

They pressed cookie cutters into the dough in silence for a minute. Melissa didn't know what to make of that, and she didn't want to ask.

"What are you going to do?" she asked Melissa.

"About what?"

Lindsay dialed it back.

"Well. Colin said the house people really want you to sell it."

"Yeah, but I need a place to live," said Melissa. Melissa looked out at the snow falling on the trees outside.

"If you sold it you could live anywhere. You could go back home, or choose a new place - California. Arizona. Italy. It gets really cold here. And it rains a lot. We're in the middle of nowhere up here. You might not like it."

She looked around at the work in progress: half-painted walls, plaster and cans of paint.

"I love it here. Besides, I've put too much into this house already. I can't leave. And when I was a little girl hearing about the Loch Ness Monster, I never imagined I'd live here. I didn't know it was possible."

"Yeah, well. You know the monster was sighted by an owner of an Inverness hotel, right? He's basically just PR."

"Don't say that," Melissa teased. "Anyway, I read that there have been stories about something in these waters since Saint Colombo."

"*Columba.* Colombo was the guy on TV in the 70s."

"Yeah. Whatever. Anyway, I've heard there've been stories for thousands of years."

"You're changing the subject. Why don't you want to go home?"

Melissa looked around her beautiful home. "It's like a fairy tale here. The old buildings, the lochs and hills. The fairy pools up in Skye - I want to visit those. And I just feel right here. And I haven't felt *right* in a long time. It's a really good feeling."

Lindsay nodded.

"Well, you're a Mackenzie. It's in your blood," she said.

"Maybe it is," said Melissa.

The buzzer rang and they took the first tray of cookies out and put the next tray in.

"I brought a bunch of candy decorations, too," said Lindsay.

"You think of everything."

"I think we're just on the same wavelength."

Lindsay spread out an array of colored candies and peppermint sticks while Melissa made the frosting.

They decorated, listening to the Christmas music, and it began to snow again.

CHAPTER 16

*M*elissa hung new Mackenzie tartan curtains while Jingles slept in his bed. Snow was falling outside and the sun glistened on it. See? It can be sunny here, thought Melissa.

Her cell phone rang. Dave's name and photo lit up the phone screen. She let it go to voice mail. When the voice mail icon lit up, she deleted it without listening.

"You and me, Jingles. We're gonna have a Merry Christmas together." Jingles wagged his tail and sat down at her feet. She wandered into the kitchen for a cookie. She glanced at a flyer she had magneted to her fridge: Highland Barn Dance.

"Oh my goodness, that's tonight," Melissa said.

She went upstairs to take a look at her dress. She had a black velvet dress and the Mackenzie tartan sash. She spent quite a while trying to get the clan pin on. She looked in the mirror and wondered whether she was dressed like a real local or like a tourist. "Here goes nothing."

When Melissa arrived, she breathed a sigh of relief: it was clear that she was going to blend in. She was one of many women dressed in a black dress with a tartan sash. Other women had tartan dresses, some had pleated tartan skirts. Others were in nice pants and a blouse. She was fine. Lindsay was right – the men looked dashing in their formal jackets and dress kilts. The barn was decorated in Christmas tartan splendor. Each table had a red velvet tablecloth with red plaid chargers and white china and silver. There were bouquets of red and white carnations, roses and greenery on each table, Christmas lights, mistletoe -- the whole place looked jolly and merry. People began to sit as elegant waiters began to bring food.

Melissa sat down at a table alone. Her phone buzzed. She silenced it and shoved it into her purse. Colin came in with his father and Lindsay. Mr. MacGregor waved and they came over to Melissa.

"May we join you, my lady?" asked Sandy with a twinkle in his eye.

"Of course," said Melissa, doing her best to keep eye contact with Sandy and avoiding Colin's eyes – he looked spectacular in his Prince Charlie jacket and kilt with a full dress sporran, clan pin, red plaid MacGregor tartan bow tie and his sparkling blue eyes.

The music started. Waiters brought plates of oat cakes and *haddie* spread.

"You're going to love the dancing," said Lindsay.

"Oh, I'm not much of a dancer," said Melissa nervously watching the locals begin to dance.

"We'll teach you," said Colin. He held out his hand. Melissa took his hand and she wondered if he, too, could feel the moment of ... something ... as they looked into each other's eyes. She flushed red, and he guided her out to the dance floor.

They joined the dancing – it was a line dance. Melissa was soon racing around, breathless, twisting under Colin's arm, moving forward to the next line of dancers, and then the next. The music was fast and fun. When the music stopped, Melissa, flushed, returned to her seat and sipped her water.

"So, what did you think?" asked Sandy.

"It's like square dancing. We did that in elementary school. The Virginia Reel."

"Yes. The pioneers in the US had learned these traditions from their ancestors and other more recent immigrants," said Colin.

Waiters arrived with a giant plate of food.

"Is this the haggis?" asked Melissa, looking at the large lump of mystery meat.

"It is," said Colin.

Melissa nodded and the waiter served the haggis, *neeps* and *tatties*.

"Whisky sauce?"

Melissa looked at Lindsay, who nodded.

"Yes, please," said Melissa.

The waiter poured whisky sauce over her haggis and served the rest of the table.

"So what exactly is haggis?"

"Try it first," said Colin.

Melissa grimaced, picked up her fork and tried it, bracing herself for the worst. Instead, she was pleasantly surprised.

"This is delicious!"

"Of course it is," said Colin with a laugh.

"And what are these? Potatoes and...?"

"*Neeps and tatties* are turnips and potatoes. Sometimes they serve it with *rumbletythump*, which has rutabaga," said Lindsay.

"And the whisky sauce is really more like gravy?"

"A bit," said Colin.

Melissa took another bite.

"There's a lot of spice," said Melissa. "What is that? Coriander?"

"That's what takes ye back to yer childhood," said Sandy, with his mouth a bit full.

"I like it," said Melissa, now eating with enthusiasm.

They watched and clapped along with the music as teenage girls performed classic dances. As dessert came around, waiters brought an array of choices to the table, served family style.

"What do we have here?" asked Melissa.

"That's Cranachan, our national dessert - raspberries and whisky, oats and cream," said Colin.

"Wow."

Lindsay pointed to a shortbread covered in caramel. "That's Millionaire Shortbread," she said.

"I can see why - look at that caramel."

"And deep-fried Mars bars," said Colin. Lindsay served everyone a bit of each.

"Delicious. You know, Colin, I can't understand why you live in the States when you have all this. The great food, your fun family..." she trailed off as the Master of Ceremonies tapped on the microphone. He was an older man, dressed in red Inverness kilt, Prince Charlie jacket and sporran.

"And now we're ready to announce the winners of the silent auction," he said as the pipe band gave a drum roll.

"The winner of the giant stuffed Santa Nessie is... Melissa Mackenzie." Melissa clapped her hands together and cheered, then ran up to collect her prize. It was huge. She could barely walk with it. She sat Nessie next to her at the table and patted it.

"Good Nessie. Good girl," she said.

"Only you would love that hideous beast." Lindsay laughed.

"I know. And I do love Nessie. I hope I see it someday."

Colin's eyes twinkled.

"Da, you want to tell her, or should I?"

"You tell it best, Da..." said Lindsay.

"Aye. Very well. When I was a lad of about twenty, my friend and I were doing some camping out near Drumnadrochit – that's out by Urquhart Castle and the deepest part of the loch." Melissa waited as he took another sip of his single malt. "Well, we were in our tent just about asleep when we heard this weird bubbling sound. We thought someone had taken out a motorboat, but it didn't sound mechanical. So we crept out of the tent and went down to the water and saw a giant fin smack – like a whale does, ken, and then dive under the water."

"And then what happened?"

"Then I woke up," Sandy said with a hearty laugh. Lindsay and Colin shook their heads. Colin held out his hand. "You could use a dance."

"Me?"

"You've got a lot to learn," he smiled.

They made their way out to the crowded dance floor.

"Your dad's quite a storyteller," said Melissa.

"That's not quite the way he always tells it. I think he actually did see something," Colin whispered while Sandy grinned and poured another glass of water.

"Well, it makes for a fun story either way," said Melissa.

The song ended and Melissa and Colin sat back down to have some coffee and after-dinner drinks. Soon people began gathering their coats and it was time to leave.

Colin walked Melissa to her car and carried that giant Nessie Santa for her. It wouldn't fit in the back seat, so they tried the trunk. That didn't work either.

"I'll put it in the truck and follow you," said Colin.

"Are you sure?"

"No worries."

"Thank you."

Snow fell as they pulled up outside the house. The lights sparkled, the moon shone on the snow-covered roof, and Melissa felt all warm and happy. Then she spotted the real estate sign.

"Why is this always here?" She hopped out of the car and struggled to pull the sign out of the frozen ground. Colin pulled into the driveway behind her and got out, Santa Nessie in his arms.

Together they tugged the sign out of the ground. They trudged through the deepening snow to the front door and found an EVICTION notice. Melissa read aloud as Colin read over her shoulder.

"Owned by the bank?" she said. "That makes no sense." Melissa tried the door. It was locked. She inserted her key. It didn't work. She turned to Colin.

"But it's my house. I've put so much work into remodeling it. All my stuff is in there," she said. "JIN-GLES IS IN THERE!" Melissa peered into the windows.

"Jingles! Jingles! Are you in there?" she called. The little dog barked.

"We've got to go in."

Colin set Nessie down on the front porch. He trudged around the side of the house toward the back door and Melissa followed.

"Do you think they changed all the locks? How can they do that?" asked Melissa.

"If they think someone is living in their property illegally, they can do it. We'll get it sorted out," said Colin as he tried the back door. It was locked.

"The garage!" said Melissa.

They trudged around to the garage, with cold, wet snow slipping into Melissa's tartan shoes as she walked.

Melissa opened the car door, pressed the remote and the garage door opened. Moments later, Melissa was inside. She looked around and breathed a sigh of relief. Everything was as she had left it -- walls partially painted, cookies in a jar on the counter.

"Jingles? Jingles! Come here, Jingles!" she called.

Jingles came trotting into the kitchen. She hugged him. While she hugged her dog, Colin was reading his phone.

"Good boy. Jingles is a good boy. Such a good, little—"

Colin put his phone back in his pocket. "I think you should stay with us tonight."

"I'll be fine here," said Melissa, thinking of all the work that still needed to be done before Christmas.

"That eviction notice is real. I'm afraid there's been some sort of scam, Melissa."

Tears welled up in her eyes. "But—"

"We'll work it out. You're tired. Gather up what you need and come stay in our guest room. We can phone the bank tomorrow."

MELISSA PACKED a bag of clothes and dog supplies and then met Colin, who was waiting at the door. On the way to the car, Melissa took one last glance around her picture-perfect dream home. The pine trees, the hill down to the loch, the deer, the beautiful old wishing well... *The wishing well!* It was her last hope.

"Colin, can you give me a minute?"

"Of course."

Melissa trudged through the snow toward the enchanting little well and stood before it. She wasn't sure what the best way to do it was, so she took a deep breath and closed her eyes.

I wish that this lovely home was mine to keep forever.

She looked down into the depths of the well and said it again. Three times seemed like a good number.

I wish that this lovely home was mine to keep forever.
I wish that this lovely home was mine to keep forever.

As she spoke the words inside her mind the third time, the wind picked up and snow from a pine tree above her fell down on her like powdered sugar from a sifter. Her eyelashes were covered in snow, but she felt a warm glow inside her. She wiped her face and, rosy-cheeked, she turned and trudged through the snow back to the sidewalk, where Colin was waiting.

"Are you all right?" Colin asked.

Melissa nodded, despite the knots in her stomach. She put her bags in the truck and got into the passenger's seat with Jingles next to her and they drove away from Greenhill House.

CHAPTER 17

*M*elissa's bleak mood began to clear as they drove into the driveway of the merrily lit MacGregor home. Melissa was grateful to have made such good friends so quickly.

Colin helped Melissa carry some things as Melissa led Jingles toward the house.

"Oh, wait. Should Jingles stay in the barn?"

"He's a house dog now. Bring him in," said Colin.

"Are you sure?"

"Aye, of course I'm sure," said Colin. Melissa wondered whether he knew the affect his Scots had on her. She guessed that maybe he did.

They shook off their snowy boots and left them by the door. Colin led Melissa down a hallway toward a spare bedroom. He put her bag down and pulled some fresh towels from a linen closet.

"The comforter's quite good, but if you get cold, there are more blankets in the hall closet," he said.

"Thank you so much," said Melissa. Jingles curled up on a little rug in the corner.

Colin turned to leave, and then turned back.

"Do you want to stay up and have a cuppa?"

"A what?"

Colin grinned. "Tea. Or hot chocolate, maybe?"

The tears were threatening to spill, but Melissa pushed them back. "Colin, you're just too nice."

"Come. Let's get you some biscuits and tea."

Melissa sat on the couch and Colin handed her his handkerchief. She blew her nose. He smiled at her.

"I'll put on the kettle."

Melissa nodded through her tears.

"Shortbread or gingersnaps?" he called from the kitchen.

Melissa croaked out something garbled – the tears were falling freely now.

"I'll bring both."

Melissa nodded, flipping through her phone. She played the voice mail.

"Melissa, this is Dave. I've finalized everything with my lawyer. He'll be in touch soon."

She sniffed and played the next message.

"Ms. Mackenzie, it has come to our attention that you have been living in Greenhill House. The home was transferred into our possession after the previous owner's death. We are upholding our possession of the home. You must vacate the premises at once. Please call us at your earliest convenience. Happy Christmas."

"Happy Christmas, indeed."

Colin returned with a pot of tea, a plate of assorted cookies and a box of tissues under his arm.

"Shall I be mother?" he asked as he reached for the teapot.

"Oh, no. I mean, I'm okay. I'm not that bad—"

"It means 'Shall I pour the tea?'" said Colin.

Melissa laughed through her tears. "Oh. Sure. I couldn't figure out what you were talking about."

He poured the tea. Melissa blew her nose.

"I'm sorry. It's just so much, all at once. At Thanksgiving I was happy and looking forward to Christmas. Now I'm getting a divorce and I'm... literally homeless."

"No, you're not, you're not, Melissa. You can stay here until you get things straightened out."

"You've already helped so much."

Before she realized what was happening, Melissa leaned in to kiss Colin. Just then Mr. MacGregor padded into the living room, breaking the spell. He saw them, grinned, and then made a show of pouring a glass of water before he returned to his bedroom. Melissa and Colin sat in another awkward silence. Colin's phone rang. He looked at it. It was Dave.

"I'm sorry - I don't know what came over me," said Melissa.

"I think I know what came over me," said Colin. He started to lean in again, but the phone rang again.

"Blast! I'm sorry, Melissa. I really must take this," said Colin.

"I understand. Good night," she said.

He looked forlorn as she went into her bedroom and shut the door.

In the bedroom she looked at a framed saying on the wall. *'Whit's fur ye'll no go past ye'.*

"I wonder if none of this is *'fur* me.'"

She laid in bed, unable to sleep. She looked at the sign again. Then she looked at a MacGregor family tree they also had on the wall. This sparked an idea. She got out her laptop and began searching. One click led to another and another...

CHAPTER 18

*S*unlight streamed through the windows, a tea kettle whistled on the stove. Eggs, square sausage, and tomatoes sizzled in a pan. Melissa came out of the guest room dressed but forlorn.

Colin flipped the fried egg and poured Melissa a cup of tea.

"Good morning," he said as he handed her the tea.

"You're all so kind. Thank you."

Once the breakfast was served, Colin sat down and looked quite serious.

"Melissa, I have some bad news. I looked into the company that sent you that original letter. Although their website is real, and they have a real office and do some legitimate business, I'm afraid their bread and butter is made by telling Americans they've inherited a home across the pond and requesting their bank account information to transfer money after a sale."

"I don't understand," said Melissa.

"It's a scam. This has happened multiple times and most of the time, it's a recently divorced or widowed woman and—"

"But I'm his long lost—"

"Mackenzie is a very common name. Especially around here. One could argue that you and the owner come from the same Mackenzie somewhere in the twelfth century. But the fact is, they selected you for your name and your situation. They wanted to scam and then rob you."

"They did. They took my house."

"Well, you see… it was never yours to begin with."

"What was the owner's name?"

"Gerald Mackenzie," said Colin.

"The letter said Stuart Mackenzie."

"See? They just make things up," he said.

"Gerald, though. That sounds familiar," she said. Melissa started to open her phone, but realized there was a gorgeous full Scottish breakfast in front of her, and politely put it away. She ate, thinking deeply, trying to puzzle something out.

Lindsay padded into the kitchen in her plaid robe and PJs.

"You're up and at 'em today," she said as she poured herself some tea.

"Gotta be ready for the tree lighting and the big party at the town green," said Melissa, hoping she sounded more cheerful than she felt.

"Definitely don't want to miss that," agreed Lindsay. Then she looked from Melissa to Colin and back, as if she was putting two and two together. Melissa flushed, as did Colin.

"I, er—"

"Melissa has a - er - problem with her house. We arrived last night and - it was best that she stayed here."

"I see..." said Lindsay with a smile as she sipped her tea.

"I brought Jingles," offered Melissa, hoping that would change the subject.

"Lovely. Does Da know?"

"About the dog in his house, or about me?"

"Which do you think he'd be more concerned about?" asked Lindsay.

Mr. MacGregor walked into the kitchen. "On the contrary, I'm thrilled on both counts. I haven't seen Colin with a woman since that—"

"Da."

Melissa blushed.

"I'm just saying, son, you've mourned long enough. It's time to move on," said Sandy.

Colin flushed and went to get more coffee. Melissa looked blankly from Mr. MacGregor to Lindsay and then Colin. What was he talking about? Lindsay looked away.

"His high school sweetheart died ten years ago. He left us. Moved to New York to be a big city barrister. He spent months retraining and learning US law. It cost a fortune. Dealing in divorce, no less. Only someone who has lost all belief in love could do that job. And having to learn the laws of a new country... he was just starting again from scratch. US and Scottish law is just so different."

"I was trying to help people," said Colin.

"By causing pain and finding a dollar amount that will solve it? And you could have helped people in Scotland. You could have moved to Glasgow, not the other side of the world."

Melissa looked away now.

"Da. I came back. I'm here. Stop punishing me," said Colin.

"I'm not punishing you. I want you here. I miss my son. You've been more yourself this past week than you have been in years. And I think..." He looked at Melissa and winked. "I think you should put your barrister skills to good use and help Ms. Mackenzie with her house situation."

Melissa wanted to crawl under the table and hide. She stood instead. "Thank you for breakfast. And for letting me stay here. I'm going to go back to the house and get the rest of my stuff. Do you know a good place for storage?"

"There's no need for that. You can store everything in our barns," said Sandy. Melissa smiled and Sandy took her hand.

"What about the animals?" asked Melissa.

"I have a feeling it'll be temporary. Colin will straighten things out," said Sandy.

CHAPTER 19

The repairs at Greenhill House had made all the difference. Melissa's Christmas decorations were picture perfect, the new paint job sparkled and the landscaping blended well with the woods and loch.

Melissa wiped a tear as she opened the garage door and went inside. The kitchen was Scottish farmhouse chic. She walked through the living room. Fresh paint, new rugs. She went into the den - still in process, but looking better. Then into the library. She took one long look out the window with its stunning view of Loch Ness. She turned to the wall of bookshelves. Something caught her eye. She climbed up the short step-ladder to retrieve it. She looked at the cover. *The History of the Mackenzie Family.* She looked at the long line of MacKenzies, dating back from the fifteenth century.

As she was about to put the book back on the shelf, a piece of paper fell out. She opened it, took a good look, and traced her finger down the line. She was stunned.

Carefully, she snapped a picture of it with her phone. Then she made a phone call.

"Hello? Yes. I'd like to request a birth certificate."

CHAPTER 20

*M*elissa, festively dressed in a Santa hat, red sweater and red jacket, joined the crowd gathering in the center of the town where the tree lighting was about to take place. Lindsay spotted her from across the street. She waved and Melissa waved back.

"How are you holding up?" Lindsay asked as she crossed over to her.

"Pretty well, actually. I've found—"

The mayor interrupted with the beginning of the ceremony. "Welcome to the annual Inverness tree lighting ceremony. We'll begin with the local pipe band, led by Sandy MacGregor."

The drumbeat started and soon anything Melissa had wanted to say was drowned out by bagpipes. She grinned at Melissa and mouthed the word "later."

Colin was a part of the procession of pipers. Melissa couldn't take her eyes off him in his kilt. But

103

just as Melissa was about to say hi, Fiona - the woman who'd gone to high school with Colin - made a beeline to Colin. She kept touching him, Melissa noticed.

"And now the moment we've been waiting for. The lighting of the tree," said the mayor. There was a drum-roll from the pipe band.

"Join me. Ten, nine..."

The crowd joined in. "Eight, seven, six..."

At the end of the countdown, the mayor flipped a switch and the tree's lights dazzled. At the same time, the whole town lit up - the stores, the street lamps, decorations over the streets and Inverness Castle.

"It's breathtaking," said Melissa.

"Right?" said Lindsay.

"Wow," said Melissa.

Carolers began singing and the crowd joined in. The Christmas parade marched by - families marched together wearing matching costumes, ugly Christmas sweaters, light up hats and more.

"Why didn't we think of that?" said Melissa.

"Next year."

Melissa looked away. Lindsay put her arm around her. "Even if we can't work things out with your house, you can get another one," said Lindsay.

Melissa blinked back tears. She had already spent too much of her own money on the renovations. If she couldn't get the house back, she was sunk.

"Let's just live in the moment, shall we? *Carpe* Christmas," she said.

"*Carpe* Christmas," said Lindsay.

They walked down the street, which glistened with colorful lights, greenery and bows. Lindsay bought light-up antlers and Christmas light necklaces and they both put them on and laughed. Some of the stores served wassail, cookies, mince pies and other treats. They gobbled them down and shopped till they dropped. Lindsay emerged with lots of packages and Melissa had a small bag of dog biscuits.

"Want to stop by my place and drop your bags and we can get ready for the party?"

"Sure."

IN THE GUEST room of the MacGregor home, Melissa's phone buzzed. Then it buzzed again. She sat up in bed and reached for her phone. It was 2 am. She had about ten text notifications.

Wanted to invite you to our New Year's Eve party. Where are you? We can't reach you.

Sending out Christmas cards - what's your new address?

Heard about you and Dave. So sorry. Call me.

Melissa smiled. Of course her friends from home hadn't forgotten her. And what seemed like a lifetime to her had only been a few weeks in reality. She had left without telling anyone of her plans - they were probably just finding out. And it was still evening in Boston. If they didn't know where she was, they didn't know how late it was.

She began texting back emojis and pictures of Scotland. She felt a warmth she hadn't felt in a while. After about a half hour, she set her phone down. But now she was awake, so she turned on her computer. Soon she was deeply absorbed on a family tree website.

MORNING SUNLIGHT SPARKLED on the snowy hills behind the MacGregor home. A flurry of baking was underway in the kitchen as Melissa and Lindsay filled trays with shortbread, bannock, and other treats. Colin and his father came in, dressed in their lumberjack finest, carrying a huge pine tree that they'd slayed.

"Cutting it a little close?" Melissa joked. "I mean, you've got hours left until Christmas."

"Just because you yanks start decking the halls in October..." bantered Colin back at her.

"Ooch. Enough. It's Christmas," said Lindsay.

"Still just Christmas Eve. Plenty of merriment ahead," said Sandy.

Colin and his father set up the tree and began checking the lights. Lindsay carried a box of ornaments into the living room. She held up the angel.

"Remember when Mum always put this up?"

"It was Gran's," said Colin.

"It was?"

"Of course. I remember it on her tree. She gave it to Mum for Christmas one year."

"And someday I'll give it to one of you," said Sandy.

They were sober for a minute as Sandy placed the angel on the top of the tree.

"Remember these birds?"

"Your mother was a loon for birds," said Sandy.

As Colin and Lindsay began to decorate the tree, Melissa stepped away. Sandy put his arm around her.

"Don't be shy, lass. We need your help."

"I just feel like everything I touch turns to—"

"Nonsense. Life is impermanent. Take a candy cane. Eat it. Enjoy. It's gone. But there will be other treats to be had." He handed her a red glass ornament.

"Colin made this when he was in school."

"It's beautiful," said Melissa.

"You should see my work in the mediums of macaroni and popsicle sticks," said Colin.

"I bet it's superb."

"Oh, yes. I was gifted from an early age. See?" He held up a Christmas tree made from popsicle sticks, pasta and paint.

"Lovely."

Soon the tree was decorated and they all sat by the fire to admire it.

"Anyone for tea and biscuits?" asked Lindsay, already heading into the kitchen.

Melissa sat there feeling awkward. "Thank you again for taking me into your home on a major holiday when I just met you."

"Lass, you're always welcome here. Now. We have a tradition in this family of opening one gift Christmas Eve and the rest on Christmas morning."

Lindsay returned with a tray of tea and shortbread. "Mum started it. Her grandmother was from Iceland, where they receive books on Christmas Eve and spend the evening reading books and eating chocolate."

Colin smiled and handed Melissa a gift.

"For me?" Melissa opened it. *The History of the Mackenzie Family of Inverness.*

"Oh my goodness. This is perfect." Melissa examined it. It was a more specific history than the book she'd found in the library at Greenhill House.

"I've seen you looking in those genealogy sites and I thought this would help fill in the gaps you can't find online."

"Thank you so much."

She handed Colin a package.

"It's not a book but it's something you can use right away," she said.

"Should I wait till tomorrow?"

"You'll want it before Christmas," said Melissa with a grin.

He opened it. It was an Ugly Christmas Jumper – complete with lights.

"For the party."

"Of course," said Colin as he held it up. "Thank you. I feel so very Americanized."

"It's you, Colin," said Lindsay.

Melissa handed Lindsay a package. It was a much cuter Ugly Christmas Jumper. And for Alexander, a light up hat. They all exchanged books and opened a box of chocolates. Soon they were all settled into their armchairs, reading and eating chocolates while the fire crackled and the snow fell.

Melissa sat up straight and gasped.

"What?" asked Colin, looking up above his book.

"You won't believe this." She opened her phone genealogy app and showed Colin her tree. "I had a hunch, so I started digging – this was back when you said Mr. Mackenzie's name was Gerald. And I dug and I dug, but I couldn't find anything. But I did find this." She handed him a slip of paper. Colin blinked. "And I thought maybe it was a coincidence. So I was trying to find proof online. But now between that, this and my own family tree—"

"What is it?" asked Lindsay.

"You really are Gerald Mackenzie's relative," said Colin.

"You are?" asked Lindsay.

"Good on you, lass," said Sandy.

"Let's ring the bank straightaway," said Colin.

"Now?"

"I'll do you one better. The owner of the bank is throwing a Christmas party tonight. Let's go," said Sandy, standing up and slipping on his shoes.

They pulled on their hats and coats and headed out the door.

WHEN THEY APPROACHED THE HOME, cars were parked on both sides of the street and festive Scottish music spilled out of the house.

"Are you sure this is okay?" asked Melissa.

"We went to grade school together," said Sandy as he walked up the sidewalk to the front door.

They went inside. Everyone was dressed in tartan, festive Christmas jumpers and light up hats. They were fine in their light-up sweaters and hats. A *ceilidh* band played, people danced and munched on mincemeat pies, cookies and punch.

Sandy set down a large hastily wrapped gift – clearly a bottle of Scotch whisky – and they all joined the party.

Colin went up to an older man in a suit, shook hands and spoke to him in a corner. The man looked over at Melissa and then came over.

"Hello, Ms. Mackenzie. Pleasure to meet you. I understand you believe you do have a claim on the Mackenzie home," he said.

"I do. If you look here, and in this book, and with these birth certificates—"

He looked at her notes and nodded. Melissa handed him the eviction notice.

"I can print them up and get them all to you. And I can get a lawyer to—"

"No need, lass. It's Christmas," said the banker. He tore up the eviction notice and grinned. "I'll still need to put things straight with our lawyers, but if your family tree works out there will be no problems."

"I think we're in need of a toast," he said.

Alexander poured them all a dram and they raised their glasses.

"*Slàinte Mhath!.*" they all said as they clinked their glasses and drank.

"To family," said Sandy.

Colin's eyes twinkled at the way his father looked at him and Melissa.

"*Alba gu bràth,*" said Melissa. They all clinked glasses. "I live in Scotland now."

"Aye, you do, lass."

And for the first time in a long, long time Melissa felt like she belonged. And it felt wonderful.

As the party ended and they put on their coats, Colin and Melissa found themselves standing in the moonlight. There was a faint green shimmer in the night sky.

"Is that the aurora borealis?"

Colin looked. "Aye, I believe it is."

"It's incredible."

They gazed at it for a long moment and then Colin pointed to the porch ceiling above: mistletoe.

"Where I come from, it's good luck to kiss under the mistletoe," he said.

"It is?"

"I just made it up. But I'm a lawyer. Want to argue with me about it?"

"Did you know that book you gave me would have the evidence I needed to keep the house?"

"I suspected that's what you were going after, but I

didn't have all your family names and dates to make the connection for certain," he said.

He looked up at the mistletoe again. "But your stall tactics would not hold up in my courtroom, Ms. Mackenzie. Are you going to do something about this mistletoe situation? I think good luck would be helpful in the new year."

"I agree, barrister."

He leaned in and kissed her.

"I think I'm already pretty lucky."

He took her hand. "Let's get you to your home."

Snow was falling steadily, and the Northern Lights shimmered. It was a perfect, magical winter wonderland as they drove along the loch toward Melissa's home. When they arrived, they each got out of the truck and stood there awkwardly for a moment.

"Well, thank you so much, Colin. For everything."

"I hope you'll come over for Christmas Day. Or we could come to your home?"

"I'd love that. Let's do both."

They heard a strange noise. A bubbling. And a splash. They looked at each other. It was coming from behind the house. They ran through the snow to the backyard. As the Christmas star shone overhead, snow fell and the Northern Lights glowed a mysterious beautiful greenish blue a strange, long rippling shape emerged from the loch. A fin shimmered in the moonlight. There was a loud splash - like a whale breeching. The ripples followed a long line in the moonlight down, deeper and deeper, down the end of the loch.

Colin raised his eyebrows.

"Was that what I think it was?" asked Melissa.

"Apparently you've got Nessie's seal of approval. You're a real Scot now. At least a real Inversnecky."

"Inversnecky? Really? Is that what they call us?"

"It's that or *Clann Na Cloiche* 'Children of the Stone' in Gaelic," said Colin, taking her hand. He leaned in.

"I haven't put up any mistletoe yet," said Melissa, still a little nervous.

"I brought my own," said Colin, holding up a sprig. Melissa laughed. "May I?"

Melissa leaned in and kissed him.

"Happy Christmas, Melissa," he said.

"Merry Christmas."

Melissa stood looking at the peaceful snowy loch. "I hate for the holidays to be over so soon," she said wistfully.

"Hogmanay's next week - the biggest, best New Year celebration you've ever seen," said Colin.

Arm in arm, they watched as -- whatever it was -- dove back into the water, swimming further and further down the lock, the moonlight glistening on its back.

THANK YOU

Hey there,

I just wanted to pop in and say a big, heartfelt thank you for joining Melissa and Colin on their adventure in *Highlands Christmas - Wishes Come True*. I hope you had as much fun reading it as I did writing it!

You know, it's like having a cozy chat by the fireplace with good friends, sharing laughs, tears, and all those warm fuzzy feelings. And speaking of warmth, that's exactly what your support brings to my heart.

If you found yourself snuggled up with the book, feeling like you were right there in the Scottish Highlands, I'd be absolutely thrilled if you could spare a moment to leave a review. It's like leaving a little love note for other readers, inviting them to experience the magic too.

Your honest thoughts mean the world to me. Did you fall head over heels for a particular scene or a quirky character? Or maybe the Highland setting whisked you away to a daydream? Whatever it is, I'd love to know!

Reviews are like the cozy blankets that keep authors going, and they help spread the word about the next book in the series, *Highlands New Year*, to even more book-loving souls.

Thank you, thank you, thank you for being part of this journey with me. Your support is the reason why I get to keep doing what I love most—telling stories.

Sending you warm hugs and endless gratitude,

Amy

COMING SOON - A SEQUEL

*G*et ready for an enchanting journey into the lives of Melissa and Colin in the upcoming Highlands Christmas Romance titled *Highlands New Year,* set to release in fall 2024. Follow their heartwarming tale as they navigate the challenges of love and life amidst the picturesque landscapes of Scotland.

Melissa finds herself at a crossroads, uncertain about her future in Scotland. Will she overcome the legal hurdles and discover a way to remain in the breathtaking country she's grown to love? An unexpected twist awaits Melissa as her dear friend from the US makes a surprise visit, determined to "rescue" her from her uncertain situation.

Meanwhile, Colin faces a difficult decision - torn between his blossoming romance with Melissa and the demands of his job back in the United States. Can their love withstand the test of distance, or will fate push them apart?

Stay tuned for *Highlands New Year,* a captivating love story that will warm your heart and leave you eagerly awaiting the magic of Christmas in the Scottish Highlands. Available for pre-order this fall.

Highlands
New Year

A HIGHLANDS CHRISTMAS ROMANCE
AMY QUICK PARRISH

ABOUT THE AUTHOR

Amy Quick Parrish is the author of multiple Amazon bestsellers, including the young adult books *Into Dust*, *Into the Storm* and *The Frequency*. This is her first Christmas book. Born and raised in Michigan, she now lives in the Boston area where she *hasnae* any sheep, border collies or hairy coos. She does have a wonderful husband and son and a lovely gray cat. She has never seen the Loch Ness monster, but her cousin who was born and raised in Inverness definitely saw something.

ALSO BY AMY QUICK PARRISH

Into Dust - The Thunderbird Chronicles Book 1
Into the Storm - The Thunderbird Chronicles Book 2
The Frequency - False Flag

Printed in Great Britain
by Amazon

30877305R00078